CLANDESTINE

AVA HARRISON

Line Edit: Write Girl Editing Services, Lawrence Editing, www.lawrenceediting.com

Content: Jennifer Roberts-Hall, Becca Mysoor

Proofreader: Love N. Books, Marla Selkow Esposito

Cover Design: By Hang Le

Formatting: Champagne Book Design

Dedicated to Melissa

You're the ying to my yang. Thank you for always being there for me. I'd be lost without you.

Exposed: *Spencer Lancaster, CEO of The Lancaster Hotels, was recently rumored to be attending clandestine meetings with UK developer Henry Gilbert. Sources close to Gilbert say Lancaster is looking to expand his currently domestic brand of hotel chains into the European market. If you recall, when the senior Lancaster retired five years ago, he snubbed his younger sons and left the hotels solely to his eldest. Spencer Lancaster appears to be anxious at the news that his estranged middle brother Grant Lancaster is starting his own brand of luxury hotels. The brothers are set to go head-to-head in a few months. Will the black sheep or the golden child playboy come out on top?*

We can't wait to report.

CHAPTER ONE

Spencer

"**F**UCKING MEDIA." THE WORDS ARE LACED WITH venom as they move past my lips. I can't believe this shit. The bastards can't keep their noses out of my business. *It's fucking bullshit.* Ever since my father named me the CEO to The Lancaster Hotel chains, they've been watching my every move.

I swear I can't catch a break. No matter where I am, they're right behind me. The constant attention from the press isn't the surprise. I'm used to it by now. But what really pisses me off is their need to constantly pit brother against brother. Pierce is too young to be part of the drama, but Grant isn't, and Grant is a major issue. The media is relentless when it comes to our estranged relationship.

We may be estranged, but that doesn't mean I don't care about him. Yes, we haven't been in the same room in years. No, we don't speak. But it doesn't mean they have to make something where it's not. Born only twelve months apart, we look almost identical with our square jaws and,

1

as the tabloids say, "piercing" green eyes, but that's where the similarities end. I'm no golden child, but I don't make dumb ass decisions all the time, *unlike my brother*.

"Mr. Lancaster?" my assistant Lucy calls from the adjoining room. "I have Gloria Reynolds on line one."

My nose scrunches at the unfamiliar name. "Who? I don't know any Gloria," I state.

"She's Mr. Gilbert's secretary, sir."

"Put her through," I bellow, grabbing the phone and pulling it to my ear. "Hello, Gloria. To what do I owe this pleasure?"

"I have Henry Gilbert holding for you. Mr. Gilbert, I have Mr. Lancaster on the line."

"Thank you, Gloria. I'll take it from here." Gilbert's thick English accent rings through the line. "Lancaster, why must your press always stick their nose in other people's business?"

"When you have the answer to that question, please share your wisdom." My eyes roll to the ceiling in frustration, and I bring my hand up to run through my hair. "What can I do for you, Henry?"

"We need to talk. Since the news has leaked that I'm looking to develop the property in Manchester, my phone has been ringing nonstop with offers."

I knew this would happen. When word got out that I was interested in that property, others would wonder what potential I saw in the location. The fact that I haven't already sealed the deal and purchased the land is a mistake

I intend to rectify.

"I hate to break it to you, but I have a string of people on the phone offering twice what you did."

Fuck, I should have known. "You wouldn't dare." The threat is thick on my tongue. Henry Gilbert got his start with my endorsement. I'd bury him as quick as I built him and he knows it.

"You're correct, champ. I'm too loyal. But Randall isn't. We both know he'd never answer your call if I weren't involved."

He's right. There has been bad blood between Randall Taylor and myself ever since a deal fell through with our fathers years ago. If it weren't for Henry's involvement and acting as the middleman between us, this deal wouldn't have even gotten this far.

"If I were you, I'd sign the papers before he goes above both our heads."

"I'm not signing shit until I see the property."

"Then I'd highly recommend that you get your arse on a plane and close the deal before I change my mind."

"I'll make my flight this afternoon. Stay in touch. I'll be in contact."

He hangs up without so much as a goodbye.

Ass.

"Lucy," I call through the door.

"Yes, sir?" Her auburn hair peeks around the frame.

"Get the plane ready. I need to fly out to Manchester."

"Absolutely. When would you like to return?"

"Tell the pilot it's one-way. I intend to work out some additional deals while in Europe."

"On it, sir." She turns to retreat.

"Lucy."

"Yes, sir." She looks at me, brow raised.

"Stop calling me sir. I'm not my father."

A smile graces her face. "As you wish."

Two hours later I'm sitting on the tarmac in one of my father's fleet of private planes. The Lancaster money and name always has its perks, and today is no exception. I'm finishing up an email to all of my hotel managers, letting them know I'll be out of town for the next couple of weeks and reminding them of the protocol when a sultry voice I've never heard before comes over the inflight speakers.

"Welcome aboard, Mr. Lancaster. My name is Victoria, and I will be at your service for the duration of our flight into Manchester. For the next eight hours, please let me know any way that I can be of assistance to you."

If she wasn't sending subliminal messages over the intercom, then I'm just a damn pervert. Everything from her voice to her words screamed, "Take me." My eyes widen when the vixen steps around the curtain that was shielding me from her view. She's new. I want to thank whoever hired her because they deserve a raise. Long black locks fall in waves down her back, and a tight black pencil skirt hugs every one of her curves. She's tall; I'd estimate five foot nine, and the violet eyes that meet mine have me ready to play. *Oh, what I can do to this woman in eight hours.*

"Mr. Lancaster. Can I get you something to drink?" she purrs.

My eyes glide over her svelte body in appreciation. The knowing smirk on her face tells me she knows what I have planned.

"Champagne, please."

She nods slowly, turning to walk away. I raise my hand, stopping her.

"Bring two glasses."

The way her lips tip up is taunting. I have no doubt the things she'll do to me will be graphic.

I can't wait.

I've been a member of the mile-high club for years, but it gets better every time. I shouldn't fuck with the staff, but I don't have any other use for her. I'm all keyed up with the possibility of losing this deal and she'll be the best distraction. I didn't get my playboy reputation for no reason.

She returns a minute later. This time I notice an extra button on her blouse is popped open. The swell of her breasts is screaming at me to touch her, to taste her, and I will. But this is a long flight and I need to take the edge off first. Accepting the glass from her hand, I take a gulp before looking up at her still standing in front of me.

"Drink," I order. She lifts her own to her mouth. *Good girl.*

When she pulls it away, she runs her tongue seductively over her lips.

"Is there anything else I can do to make your flight more

enjoyable?" Her tongue juts out and there's no mistaking the question she's asking. I'm only too happy to oblige. My glass hits the table with a thud and her lip tips up at the gesture.

"I'm sure you can think of something . . ." The words hang in the air as an invitation. But I won't clarify.

I'm Spencer Lancaster.

I don't have to.

Without another word, she sets her own glass down and drops to the floor in front of me. Reclining back, I look down at her as she begins to crawl toward my seat.

The view is fantastic.

"Unzip me," I demand and then watch through hooded lids as she arranges herself on the floor, leaning over me. Her eyes never leave mine as she pulls me from the tight confines of my pants. Stroking me up and down, I let out a groan of satisfaction when the warmth of her mouth engulfs me.

Perfect.

Absolutely fucking perfect.

At thirty-six thousand feet, I imagine this is pretty fucking close to what heaven must feel like.

With her hand and mouth working in perfect symphony, it's a mere matter of minutes before my balls tighten and I know my impending release is imminent. Normally I'd warn her, but seeing as she's made it clear she's here for my enjoyment, I just close my eyes and allow myself the blissful relaxation she's offered.

CHAPTER TWO

Olivia

CAN'T BREATHE.

My racing heart makes it hard to keep still as I wait. *Torture.* It feels like I'm having a heart attack, but I know I'm not. It's only anxiety.

A fear of what's about to happen. The fear of the unknown.

Today has got to go down in history as one of the worst days of my life. It was utter hell. I've been baking in the hot sun in a tiny bikini, and now I have sand in places it should never be. All I want is a huge glass of water and a nice cold shower. Instead, I'm stuck sitting here waiting inside the lobby outside of Giorgio, my photographer's office, as he's requested. Even the thought of it makes my shoulders tense and a sick feeling coils in my belly. This can't be good, as Giorgio never sees models after shoots.

The shoot.

The dreadful shoot, I should say.

He was not happy at our photo shoot. It was obvious in

the way his body was rigid every time he looked through the lens. With each shot he took, he'd look down at the image on the camera and his brows would draw together. His heavy sighs, and the fact that he damn near chucked his camera across the beach, were sure signs that something's up.

I look at the poster on the wall next to me. A stunning blonde is sprawled out across the beach in a bikini that just barely covers her breasts. She's thinner than I am, her bones jutting out from her hips. I used to look like her. Unhealthy. That was back when I was anorexic. I drank my meals and snorted my dessert. It almost killed me. I was so thin that my ribs were on display. I'll never go back to that again. Now at twenty-four, I have more curves than I ever did before. Guys love curves, though, right? Not that it matters what they like. *I'm still alone.*

Running a hand through my blond locks, I decide it's time to knock again. I manage a deep breath as I stand; counting slowly to ten and allowing each inhale to calm my fragile nerves. With a tentative lift of my hand, I knock, this time desperately hoping I'm overreacting and when he does answer, I'll find relief.

"Olivia." My name is screamed from the other side of the door. "Come in," Giorgio commands.

I stand on wobbly legs and walk toward Giorgio's office. I can hear his thick Italian accent, but I don't know the words. I turn the knob and the door creaks open. My head slowly peeks in.

"You wanted to see me?" I squeak. My stomach turns with the anxiety of what he wants to say to me. It feels like my heart might hammer out of my chest any minute.

"Take a seat, Olivia." He gestures to the chair in front of him.

With slow, hesitant steps, I sit.

We're quiet for several moments, which does nothing to help calm my nerves. I watch him with acute awareness, pulling in oxygen slowly so I don't hyperventilate. I hate confrontation. It makes me feel as though my breath has been cut off as I wait for him to speak, to confront the issues he has with me. The silence is heavy in the air. It envelops the room, and I wait for any sign that he'll break it. Finally, his eyes grow weary, and I know it's time.

His tone is soft when he says, "Your body has changed."

My brow furrows. "What do you mean, Giorgio?" I know exactly what he means. I'm not like the girl on the poster outside, but I want to hear him say it.

"I'm only saying that things are different from the last time we shot photos."

"What you're not saying is you think I'm fat."

He shakes his head violently at that. "Olivia, you know I'd never say that."

Of course, he wouldn't. That would be grounds for a lawsuit. But he thinks it regardless, and suddenly I'm remembering one of my first photo shoots with my ex-boyfriend Bennett. *"Your thighs. They shouldn't touch. That needs to be fixed."*

No, I won't allow myself to go there. If I do, the realization that I'm not *perfect* will tear me apart. So instead of thinking about it, I focus my anger and pin him with my most heated glare, causing him to flinch. Unlike many of the other photographers, Giorgio is tenderhearted, but it appears he's no different from any of them. All he see's is every single flaw on my body and knowing that makes me want to wrap my arms around myself and hide from his scrutiny.

"I'm only saying that you don't look healthy and I'm concerned."

I scoff at that. "Your idea of healthy and mine are two very different things, Giorgio. I, for one, don't think that bones protruding from someone's body are healthy."

"You have your opinion, and I have mine." He shrugs. "Our readers have been polled for numerous years, and the fact of the matter is they want something that you aren't."

"Are you letting me go? We still have three more locations to shoot," I cry. I don't want to fail. I don't want to admit this has all been a big mistake. That I was and still am not good enough. My stomach begins to tighten as a familiar need to numb the pain claws through my veins.

"You know I love working with you, Olivia. You've always been one of my favorites. But you were hired by Soleil for their calendar because you *had* a specific look." *Rail thin with breasts.* He doesn't have to say it. I know how I became a model. I know what Bennett saw in me.

"Seeing as you no longer fit the look for this campaign, I'm going to have to dismiss you from the rest of the shoots. You need to go and do some soul-searching and figure out if this is still what you really want."

Anger seeps into my being. "Giorgio, cut the shit. Say what you mean."

He huffs out a long breath before placing his hand over his eyes, thinking of what to say. "If you ever want to work again, you'll need to go tone up and get back to where you were two years ago."

I knew what he would say, but knowing doesn't take away the hurt once he says them. His words cut deep.

Two years ago.

A miserable haze I can barely remember . . .

Anorexic and using cocaine.

A dark, painful spiral I barely escaped. I can't go there again. As hard as I try, and as angry as I was seconds ago, I can't stop the waterworks. Tears begin cascading down my cheeks.

With nothing more to say, I stand and begin my walk of shame.

Twenty long minutes later, I'm finally home. As I begin to push open the door to the apartment, my phone begins to ring. *Shit.* It's Helen, my agent. Helen took me on as a client after my career took a nosedive two years ago. When not one other agency would touch me with a ten-foot pole, Helen believed in me.

"Hi," I huff into the phone as I open the door to my

apartment. Placing my bag down, I move into my living room. "I guess you heard the news." There is no hiding the groan in my voice.

"Yes, I did." My stomach sinks at the cool detachment in her words. "I'm going to give it to you straight. I can no longer book you on high profile jobs. The only thing you'll be able to get is catalog work, not high-end couture."

"But you don't rep catalog models." Please don't cut me loose. *Please say you'll make an exception for me.*

"No, I don't," she says with finality, and that's when I realize the other shoe has officially dropped. Helen no longer believes in me.

I'm not good enough.

Maybe I never was . . .

CHAPTER THREE

Olivia

J OBLESS.

Worthless.

Not good enough.

The words are a heavy burden on me. Casting a shadow that crushes my ribs, making it hard to breathe.

What the hell am I going to do now?

Technically, I don't need the money to live, but if I'm not a model, who am I?

Modeling was never about money for me. It was about pride. Being good at something. It was about my self-worth. I thought I'd be able to be healthy and be successful, but I was wrong.

Now what? This is the second time in my life I don't know what I'm going to do with myself. I want to be strong but the need to drown myself in a haze of booze and drugs is overpowering.

I reach for my phone.

Me: I wish you were here. I need to go out!

Lindsey: Really?

Me: Yeah! My life is over.

Lindsey: Over-dramatic much?

Me: I was fired.

Lindsey: Fired from what gig?

Me: All gigs. I'm no longer a model.

Lindsey: I'm sure it's not that bad.

Me: No it's worse. I have no prospect. Nothing.

Lindsey: Meet me in London. Crash at my place. I know a few agencies and photographers here. I'll put out some feelers.

Me: You'd do that?

Lindsey: Sure thing, Chica! It's boring here without you.

This will be a perfect way to distract myself.

"Drink up, bitches," Lindsey, my loud and boisterous friend, calls across the table, handing me our third shot of Patrón.

It's been a week since I was let go from the photo shoot, and every day has been the same foggy mirage. Wake, nurse a hangover, begin drinking again, and then off to the clubs. Every damn day. The only positive? I haven't succumbed entirely to my old habits. My body is still cocaine free—which is a small miracle these days, but I won't allow myself to go there.

No. I can't.

Still, I can't help but to eye the liquid sitting in my hand, knowing full well I should put it down. Knowing that this isn't supposed to be my life anymore. I gave this up, and I've tried my hardest for the past two years to not fall back into these habits. But Giorgio's words ring in my ear even a week later, I need to lose weight in order to model, but that comes with a price. The only way for me to lose weight in that short of time is to forget the promise I made to myself. I have to be weak. And it kills me a little inside to even consider it.

I'll have to sell my soul to get another agent.

"Liv, bottoms up. What are you waiting for?" Lindsey quirks her left eyebrow up at me in question.

This is the first time we've been together in months. Lindsey had a fight with her parents and hopped a plane to Europe. It's funny how she didn't skip a beat the second I texted her. She doesn't even care that we haven't spoken since she went abroad. Wherever the party is, Lindsey follows. She has no intentions of changing that anytime soon. Heir to an oil empire, she wants for nothing but attention. Her life comes with no stipulations or requirements other than age and the death of her parents. The thought of aging kills Lindsey, but parents dying doesn't faze her. She counts down the days.

We each have our own story as to why we got into the party life. For her, it was a lack of attention. Her parents were never around to stop her. For me, it was the opposite.

My parents were pretty much the most perfect parents ever. It's exhausting how perfect they are.

Making myself that perfect is also exhausting.

But that's not why I started down this path. It wasn't until *modeling* that I was introduced to all these vices. I was never skinny enough. Never pretty enough. Never *enough*.

"Seriously, Olivia, I'm bored. Are you going to drink or should we call it a night?"

Lindsey's annoyed tone has me snapping my attention back to her. Her arms are lifted in the air, her face scrunched. *Not good enough for her time.* A cold knot forms in my stomach at the thought. Mustering all the energy I have, I shake off the feelings threatening to wreak havoc to my night.

"Cheers," I say, lifting my shot in the air to her and the rest of our friends who have gathered around us to also take a shot. With a tip of the glass, the liquid burns my throat as it goes down. I want to cough, but I hold it in. I don't want to appear weak in front of these people. I call them my friends, but they're not. The second I'm no longer fun, they'll find something better to do. It's exactly why I haven't spoken to Lindsey since she moved to London. She doesn't care about me. This life is full of nothing but fake people, and in my circle, she's the queen.

"That's my girl," she squeals. "Who wants another?" Lindsey asks, not really caring. She's already bouncing her way back up to the bar. I scowl at her back.

"You okay?" the girl Lindsey introduced to me earlier tonight named Amelia says. Her voice is a little above a whisper. There's sincerity in her voice that I'm not used to in this world. A sincerity that reminds me of home. Of my sisters. It makes my heart squeeze in my chest.

Looking at Amelia, she reminds me so much of myself before I became engulfed in this world. She looks so innocent like a young calf about to be slaughtered. She's new to this group. I wish I were brave enough to tell her to run, that these people will only ruin her, but I don't say those things.

"I'm good. Are you having fun?" I change the topic back to her, not having any desire to talk about everything that's hanging over me right now.

"Yeah. Sure. I guess." She bites her lip before continuing. "I'm not really into clubbing."

My head tilts. "How did you meet Lindsey?" My curiosity is piqued. This girl doesn't seem at all like the type Lindsey would hang out with.

"I'm Lindsey's cousin. I'm here visiting for the summer."

I nod. It makes sense now. Poor girl. "She'll have you hopping all over the globe, chasing one party after another."

Amelia grunts. "That's what I'm afraid of. I hate this." She sits back in her chair. Her cheeks draw in as her skin pales. She's looking a bit green like she might throw up.

"If you don't want to be here, you could always go

home," I suggest. If it were me, I would.

Lie.

"Right. Like she'll allow that." She exhales a long breath, her shoulders sinking forward. "If I go home, my uncle will put me on the first flight back to Indiana and I'd rather be anywhere but there."

There's a story there, but I won't press. Whatever it is, she's clearly running from it. It's her business, and if I'm honest, I don't want to start getting personal as I have a mountain of things I for sure don't want to talk about.

"Why are you here?" Her question catches me off guard.

"I haven't seen Lindsey in a while, and I needed to let loose."

Her brow rises. Not buying what I'm selling. "You don't seem to like Lindsey all too much."

Am I that transparent? Clearly, I am or Amelia is very perceptive. I need to do a better job at hiding my feelings or I'll find myself alone. I already lost so many friends when my career tanked. Lindsey is one of the only reminding friends I have left, I can't afford to lose her too. But with the alcohol coursing through my veins, it seems impossible to rein in my true feelings.

"I like her just fine. I'm not in the mood tonight." Looking off in the opposite direction, I try to distance myself from this conversation. This is not the time or place nor do I know Amelia well enough to disclose my feelings. Lucky for me, Lindsey returns in the nick of time, sauntering back over to us with a hand full of shots.

"Here you go. Patrón number two," she calls out. We take the small glasses in our hands.

"That would be number four," Amelia corrects, causing her to receive Lindsey's glare.

"I don't care. Take the shot," Lindsey orders, no room for objections.

Amelia and I both do as we're told, lifting the shot to our mouths and slamming them home. Liquid fire burns my throat. Like battery acid, it leaves an imprint even after all the fluid has been consumed. That is not tequila.

What the fuck?

Shaking my head back and forth, I try to rush the horrible sensation to pass. Lindsey's cackle is heard over the booming bass of the DJ.

"What was that?" Amelia asks between gags.

"Absinthe," Lindsey replies with a shrug. "The hot bartender let me sneak him a bottle." She lifts her chin in acknowledgment to the man behind the bar.

My jaw tightens at her words, every muscle in my back becoming rigid. "Why the hell would you do that? You know that shit makes me stupid," I hiss.

Lindsey tips her lips up into her signature smirk. She doesn't care. She only cares about herself. "Yeah, well, you needed to lighten up. This is a step in the right direction. Here take this." She hands me a full glass of clear liquid. I stare at it intently. "Chill out. It's only vodka."

I hate her. I hate this scene.

So why are you here?

I'm here because these people will help me forget my pathetic life for a little while. *Is your life really that bad? A family who loves you . . .*

But you're not good enough.

You're not like them.

You can't go back.

My lips start to move, trying to fire back, but the way Lindsey's eyes widen marginally has me shutting my mouth before I speak. She smiles at that, knowing she won. With an audible sigh, I try again, but this time my words are lost in my mouth.

Out of nowhere Lindsey grabs my free hand and pulls me to follow her. When we move a few feet through the crowd, I see that our friend Murphy is leaning down in a far booth in the corner. He's about to take a bump of coke. He bends lower, trying to be discreet, but there's no mistaking what he's doing, the bronze key lifting up to meet his nostril. A part of me wants to beg him to give me a taste too.

But I don't.

Instead I down my drink in one gulp, staving off the hunger that always grows when I see it.

He looks back up, and his eyes lock with Lindsey. His face splits in a sinister smile as he lifts his hand and points for us to come over.

Shit.

"Come on, let's sit at his table."

"Do we have to?" I mumble so low there's no way she can

hear me over the boom of the bass. The temptation will be too much to bear. But I have no choice. Lindsey is already pulling me over.

Within an hour, Lindsey and I are drunk. Very drunk, and we're dancing on the bench of the banquette in the club.

"God, I love having you here. This is so fun. I can always count on you to come around and have fun, even if you're a brat at first."

I want to object and say I'm not a brat, but truth be told, I'm too drunk to care. "Things are never dull when you're around." Lindsey grins. "Come on. Let's do some more shots."

The rest of the night is a blur. I decide to drink everything Lindsey puts in front of me, and at some point, everything becomes a hazy mess.

Eventually my vision goes black.

———————————————

The next morning, I awake with the same terrible headache I had the day before. A loud, pained croak escapes my lips. The need for coffee is very real. When I'm seated at the table about to take my first sip of the much-needed caffeine, Lindsey comes in the room laughing. She slams a magazine down on the table. "When you come to town you go big. I'll give you that."

I look down to see my face gracing the cover of the *Expositor*. It's a sister division of the tabloid *Exposé* in the

United States.

Exposed: The Oil Heiress is at again.

Lindsey Walker was spotted last night dancing on tables with her favorite gal pal Olivia Miller.

If the name sounds familiar, it should. Miller got herself in a heap load of trouble a few years back.

These two together can only mean bad things . . .

We can't wait to report.

The picture has me cringing. The way my dress pulls against my torso, shows every ripple of my body but not in a good way. My jaw looks flat. Not my best angle. And to make it even worse, I look like I'm high as a kite. I'm not, but that's not how it looks. There's picture after picture of me chugging shots, and I'm instantly sick to my stomach.

In my head, I can hear Bennett's words.

Search for the best light.

Never angle that way. It makes you look fat.

You don't need to drink that. It will only make you gain weight.

"Oh, come on, Olivia. It's not that bad. We've all made the *Expositor*." She absently picks at her nails. "It means you're back in the game," she exclaims. "We need to cele-brate." She skips off.

My head falls to my hands, ashamed. I set out to forget, but I didn't want to end up back in the tabloids. One of the things I've prided myself on the past couple of years is restoring my name. This crowd will tarnish my reputation quickly. The fact that Helen was even willing to take a chance on me after my fall from grace was a once-in-a-lifetime thing. She saw something in me that I didn't. But that was twenty pounds ago. Back when I was in the best shape of my life. *Bones sticking out and all.*

But now, with this cover, everyone will think I'm back to my old ways on top of the fact that my body is no longer what it was . . . yeah, I've definitely put the nail in my coffin.

I knew my modeling days were probably over before I came to London, but there was still that little sliver of hope that maybe, somehow, I'd figure out a way to come back. But not after this. There's no way.

It's over. It really truly is over this time. I've no idea what I'm going to do. I'm going to have to go home with my tail tucked between my legs and face my family, which I've avoided for a long time. As supportive as they were my whole life, modeling was nothing they could stand behind. To them, it was beneath us.

Not that they can say anything. My shenanigans are just some on the long list of the indiscretions of the Miller family. When I was little, my father was never around, and when my mom finally told him to get out, he started an affair, which resulted in a half-sister, Lynn. We didn't find out about her until my third year in college. Lynn carried on a lengthy affair with her teacher, but now they're together. *Happy.*

Then there's my sister Bridget. We share both parents, but you'd never be able to tell. She's much more like Lynn than me. Perfect. Beautiful. They seemed to have inherited all of our father's good genes. I got the reject ones. The ones that made his marriage fail.

The drinking. The partying. The sex.

Yeah, I was destined to be a mess. Regardless, I always wanted something different. I wanted to make my family proud. I'm not smart like my surgeon father, or incredibly outgoing like my sisters and mother, but I hoped that superficially I could shine. And I did. *For a while.*

There is no saving my career now. I'm not even sure I should bother going to the meeting Lindsey set up for me tonight with her contacts. *Why bother?* No. I at least have to try.

"Lindsey," I yell.

"Yeah?" She pokes her head around the corner.

"I have that meeting tonight, so I won't be able to hang out. I'm also going to pack up and try to get out of here tomorrow. So, I probably won't see you before I leave."

"Oh?" She raises her brow.

"I'll call you if I'm back in town."

She frowns and then disappears again. I sound like an ungrateful bitch. She did help me, but I just can't be here right now. I need to at least try to make plans for my future. I know I can't do that here partying with Lindsey.

Maybe I'll get lucky and this agent will like me. Maybe someone will believe in me again and my life doesn't have to be like this anymore.

CHAPTER FOUR

Spencer

"YOU'VE GOT TO BE FUCKING KIDDING ME." I begin to pace back and forth, my fist clenching and unclenching. *How the hell did this happen?* "You had me fly all the way out here just so you could tell me that you sold it out from underneath me?"

"Spencer, mate, calm down. It wasn't mine to sell. You know that." He lets out an anxious cough before pulling at his hair as he searches for a way to defuse the situation.

I'm not having it, though.

"Bullshit," I seethe, and he flinches at the sound of my voice. "You were supposed to have everything ready to go for me when I got here. You know I'm more than good for the funds."

"It's not about that. The buyer offered more and Randall accepted." Henry runs his hand back through his graying hair.

"What happened to a man's word? You told me he

wasn't looking to sell, but he'd sell to us for the price we negotiated. What the hell happened?"

"He changed his mind. A better offer came around." Henry shrugs wearily.

"Fuck this. I'll bury him."

"This is business, Spencer. It's not personal. Let's not get carried away. I told you there were a lot of offers once the news got out."

"You know I would've matched anything."

"Funny, that's exactly what the new buyer said." He sighs. "In fact, he promised to outbid anything that you did by at least a mil."

I scoff. Who the hell would do that? If I'm being honest, I wouldn't have paid much more than my offer.

As if reading my mind, Henry adds, "You didn't want this land that bad anyway or this deal would've been done months ago."

I don't comment. "Who bought it?"

"I don't know. They wanted to remain anonymous. Randall wouldn't tell me."

"Are you the developer?" I level Henry with my most heated stare.

"You know I am." His voice is defeated.

"We're done. I won't ever work with you again."

"Bloody hell, I figured you'd react like this." He throws his hands up in the air. "What did you want me to do? I can't walk away from a project right now."

"Listen to me, you fuck. We had an agreement. An

26

understanding. You shitting all over *my* deal is going to have some consequence."

"I had to take it. I don't have those luxuries right now, Spencer. You know I don't," he mumbles. His face is pale and his eyes are wide. If I'm not mistaken, a bead of sweat is collecting on the side of his face. He's scared. *Rightfully so.* He should be. I clench my jaw, and he shudders as he waits for me to say more, but I'm done with him. When it becomes painfully obvious by the silence in the air, the pussy turns his back and walks away like the coward he is.

But he was right about one thing. I wasn't necessarily bought into that property. There were a lot of downsides to it. The location was subpar. There were dilapidated buildings that would need to be demolished, which would have driven up the costs. If I'm being honest, whoever bought the property did me a favor.

But I don't like to lose.

I need to get the hell out of Manchester. Maybe I'll have better luck in London.

———————

I've been sitting in the hotel lobby bar at what is known to be the "hottest" hotel in London for the past hour nursing a tumbler of Johnnie Walker Blue Label and making plans. Knowing the competition is important when expanding into a new region, so that's what I'm doing. I came to buy a property, and I'm not leaving Europe until I do. The future of Lancaster Hotels depends on an international expansion. My father was stuck in his ways and did nothing. Once I took over however, he finally admitted he was wrong. I won't let him down. Not after all the trust he's put in me.

I'm about to call it a night and head to my penthouse to do research when a beautiful blonde walks in and sits four seats down from me.

She doesn't look at me. Not. Once.

I'm a cocky bastard, and I won't apologize for it. Women love me. Well, they love my money. I'm Fortunes Businessperson of the Year. I made Forbes 40 Under 40. I was People's Sexiest Man this year and listed on Cosmopolitan's 50 Hottest Bachelors. I'm a big fucking deal, and this woman didn't even look twice.

I look her over, unabashed. There's something familiar about her, but I can't put my finger on it. I'm good with faces, and if I really searched hard, I'd recall it, but the truth is, it doesn't matter who she is right now. I'm intrigued regardless.

Her long, tanned legs are crossed at the knee, and the white lacy dress she wears hikes up on the side, showing a good portion of her toned thigh. My gaze moves up her torso, stopping at her exposed neck. There's something sensual about a woman's neck. I bet if I leaned in and ran my nose up to her ear, she'd quiver under my touch.

Her golden locks hang over the opposite shoulder in light waves. I can't see her eyes, and it's probably a good thing or she'd know just how brazenly I'm staring.

What the fuck is wrong with me? It's not like I didn't just get laid. I can't even blame that for my lack of propriety. A steady stream of one-night stands should be keeping me sated. Maybe I need something more?

No.

The last fling I embarked on that was longer than a few nights ended badly. No matter how many times I told her I wasn't looking for anything serious, she didn't listen. In the end, when I said it would be our last night together, she hurled a red-soled stiletto at my head. I haven't had the time nor inclination to engage in another affair.

"Can I get you another, sir?" The bartender leans too far over the bar, making sure my eyes are level with her robust cleavage.

I should say no. I need to do work and hit the sack, but I don't. Instead, my gaze finds the beautiful blonde at the end of the bar again.

Blue eyes. Full red lips.

Breathtaking.

I internally smack myself, needing to pull it together. I've seen plenty of pretty women in my life, and I'm no longer a hormonal teenager. I'm about to order her a drink when she glances down at her phone and then abruptly leaves the bar. *Damn shame.*

"Another?" the bartender says, pulling me out of my dirty thoughts.

"Yep." I'll need a whole bunch more to turn this crap

day around. *Or a distraction.* Scanning the bar, I look for one. Not one of the women still left in the room holds a candle to the blonde.

The bartender sets my scotch down and I make work on it. Half way through the glass, my phone buzzes in my pocket. It's a text from my assistant.

Lucy: Pierce is in London.

Great. Just what I fucking need. With one gulp I empty the glass and stand. I need a damn cigarette, but having to walk through the hotel lobby and out the front door is out of the question. I don't want to speak to anyone. There's got to be a better place.

"Closest exit? One where I won't be bothered," I ask the bartender as I hold up my cigarette.

"There's a private area right down the hall for the staff to take a break. I'm sure no one would mind if you use it, Mr. Lancaster." I smile at that. Of course they wouldn't. *They know who I am.*

Making my way out of the bar and down the hall opposite the lobby, I see a door with the words Staff Only. I push it open and find that the bartender is wrong. I'm not alone. Standing against the wall is the blonde from the bar.

It seems my night might be turning around.

"I'm pretty sure this area is only for the staff," I say to her.

"How do you know I don't work here?" Her American accent catches me off guard. I expected something else.

Because of her hair and eyes, I thought she'd be Swedish.

"Looking at your clothes, it's obvious."

A small twitch in her cheek tells me she wants to smile, but instead, she purses her lips and runs her hands over her dress showing just how much it clings to her perfect body. "And what's wrong with my attire?"

I raise an eyebrow. "It's rather short, don't you think?" It's the perfect length in truth. Short enough that if I fuck her right here in the back alley, it won't get in the way.

"It has to be."

"And why is that?" This I'm interested in hearing.

"It needs to be short enough to show off my new shoes." She winks.

With that, I let out a hearty laugh all while I let myself trace her legs with my eyes until I see that she's wearing a pair of sexy as fuck shoes. I imagine them digging into my back as I press into my bed and have my way with her. Pulling my gaze back up I meet her stare.

She gives me a coy smile. Her teeth are biting her lower lip. Her pupils are large and the way she looks at me, I knew if I wanted to, I could push her against the wall right here and now.

"You're trouble."

"You have no idea."

"Well, they definitely call attention to your . . ." I smirk at her. "Shoes."

She doesn't answer, just takes a drag of her cigarette. The action calls attention to her full lips. Lips I'd like to kiss right now.

I pull out my own cigarette then start searching for a match.

"Here." She walks closer to me, her hand extending to light me up. I use the small move as an excuse to brush my finger against her skin. To see how she'll react to my touch. When I see her noticeable shudder, satisfaction courses through me. Good. I like that she's affected by me.

"I don't usually smoke." I shrug. "But it's been that type of day."

"I hear you."

Just as I take my first puff, she snuffs hers out and then moves closer to the door. "Thanks for keeping me company," she says over her shoulder.

"It was my pleasure . . ." I open the door for her. "I hope we meet again." And I do, but next time I hope she's naked and bent over the arm of the couch in my suite.

I take a few more drags before throwing it to the ground and stomping on it. As luck will have it, when I enter the bar she's back to sitting in the same spot as before.

"Join me," I say across the bar.

She stands and sits in the seat beside mine. "Hi." She extends her hand in introduction and I take it in mine.

"I'm—"

"Nope," she interrupts all while shaking her head.

"No name?" I inquire.

"Nope." She puckers her lips in a flirtatious manner.

"It's more fun this way." She winks, and I laugh. *No name.* I'm okay with that. More than okay, actually. Her handshake is firm, but her skin is silky soft.

"Well, then nice to meet you." I level her with my sexiest smolder. She appears unaffected. What the fuck? "Drink?"

She nods, and I motion to the bartender to get us another round. When the martini is placed in front of her, she turns to me.

"Thank you." I watch as her lips touch the glass. My pants tighten and I have to shift to get comfortable. "Where are you from?" she asks me, and I clear my throat at her question, trying to compose myself.

"New York. You?"

"The same." She draws out the words, looking at me closer. "You look familiar," she appraises.

"I get that often. What brings you to London?" I ask, steering the conversation back to safe ground.

"I was involved in a photo shoot, but it ended. So I flew here."

"Ah. Model." She doesn't look like any models I know, and I know my fair share. This girl is curvaceous and stunning. She's also down-to-earth and funny. Traits I rarely find in models.

"Was. It doesn't seem to be working out well for me."

I raise a brow.

"I've just parted ways with my agency and was supposed to meet a guy here for another job opportunity, but he seems to have stood me up."

"His loss." Our eyes lock, my mouth parting into a smirk. "My gain."

She smiles and I swear the fucking wind is knocked out of me. She's gorgeous. Not the fake, overtly sexual girls I'm used to. No, she's demure, sophisticated, utterly fucking gorgeous. She blushes under my scrutiny and I can't help but grin.

We both reach for our drinks, tipping it back faster than the first. "What about you? What brings you to London?"

"Business, but I don't want to talk about me. I want to hear more about you."

"What do you want to know?" By the way her cheeks sink in and the small line forming between her brows, I can tell she doesn't want to impart any personal information. That's how I like it.

"Are you in London alone?"

"I met friends here."

"And where are these friends now?"

"Don't know. Don't care. I'm happy right where I am."

I like her answer. I move closer, placing my hand on the back of her chair. My finger grazes her exposed skin, and she lets out an audible sigh at the touch. *Good.* After Manchester, she's exactly the distraction I need. She doesn't care who I am. Doesn't seem hell-bent on chaining a ball to my leg, which is just the kind of girl I'm interested in.

"I like that."

"Like what?"

"That you don't care what people think."

She takes the rest of her cocktail in one more sip. "And I like this drink." She winks, and I can't help but laugh. "So are we going to have another?" Her lip tips up into a smirk and it's by far the sexiest thing I have ever seen. She's so different from the women I know. It's refreshing.

"Another round," I say to the bartender then turn back to the intriguing stranger. "Have you ever been here before?"

"Is that the best line you got?"

"Beautiful, I don't need any lines." I return her smirk with my own. "If I want you, I'll have you."

"Oh is that so?"

My finger presses once more onto her flesh, and this time I'm met with a wave of goose bumps. I lean close to whisper into her ear, so close I can almost taste her skin. "I always get what I want."

And I do.

And I want her.

By cocktail number four I'm feeling good and ready to take this somewhere a little more private. "Would you like to come up to my room for one more drink?" I hang the invitation in the air, hoping she'll oblige.

She studies me closely. "One more drink?" she probes.

"One . . . or more if you like."

Her tongue darts out, wetting her bottom lip, and I

imagine what that tongue would feel like if she took me in her mouth. I feel myself harden to the point of pain. *Fuck.* I'm losing what little control I have left.

"Okay."

CHAPTER FIVE

Olivia

'M IN THE SEXUALLY CHARGED, OVERTLY TIGHT CONFINES of an elevator, with *the* Spencer Lancaster.

Of course I know who he is. It's not as if I'm a yearly subscription holder to *Cosmopolitan* or anything. He's the hard ass CEO who every single socialite in New York City is supposedly after. I'd never admit to him that I know who he is. From what I understand, the playboy has an ego that needs to be popped.

I ignored him when I first entered the bar for that reason. I don't like arrogant assholes, and I know his reputation is just that. Asshole is not something I need to get tangled up in. But, I found him to be . . . different. So far he's been completely down-to-earth and even charming.

That is how I find myself standing a mere two inches away from one of the best looking men I've seen in my life. The electrical charges pulsing between us are maddening. It's a heady and foreign feeling. I've never fawned over a man. Ever. Spencer Lancaster is proving to challenge me.

"Don't," he says roughly.

I look at him, eyebrow raised. "Don't what?"

"You know what." He stares at me with the intensity of a blazing inferno and I'm waiting for him to reach out and engulf me in flames.

"If you keep looking at me like that, I'll take you right here in this elevator," he growls.

Tingles run down my body. He's a gorgeous man. I'll admit. But that hasn't ever been enough to incite these types of reactions in me. He's turning my world on its side in a matter of minutes, and at this very second I want to tip over the edge so he'll keep his promise and take me right here, so I do my signature move, dashing my tongue out and swiping at my bottom lip slowly and seductively.

Faster than I can comprehend, he's pushing my back up against the wall. His lips hover over mine as he runs his hand up my side, stopping right below my breast. I whimper at his touch. A groan escapes him at our connection, but he doesn't kiss me. Just hovers, letting his breath tickle against my skin.

"Say you want this," he demands as he pushes my dress farther up my thighs, exposing the fact that I'm not wearing panties.

"Yes. I want this."

He growls. The rough pads of his fingers grasp at my skin.

Teasing me.

Leaving bruises.

Desperate to touch me, to be inside me.

They get closer and closer.

The anticipation is torture, all-consuming as I mentally beg for him to breach me.

My breath comes out in shallow bursts.

The tip of his finger is there. Lifting my hips up, I try to bridge the gap, but just as he begins to dip inside, the elevator pings, notifying us we've reached the top floor. He doesn't disconnect from me. Instead, he moves us backward out of the elevator, only stopping when we've reached his door. He pulls the key hurriedly from his pocket, opening the door and ushering me inside.

I'm barely over the threshold when I'm spun around, back hitting the wall. His hands run up my body. His gaze glides over me hungrily. He leans in, placing his nose in the crook of my neck, and tingles race across my body at the simple touch.

My lips part in a silent invitation for him to taste my mouth, he moves away from me and answers my invitation, accepting with a vigor that's unsurpassed. It's not soft or silent. It's frenzied and primal.

We separate for a breath but then he grabs me, pulling me back to him, slamming his mouth back to mine. With his free hand, he lifts my jaw to deepen the kiss. Now with no space between us, I can feel the hard planes of his body against mine. I can feel the beat of his heart, the breath in his lungs, the passion in his veins. He's desperate for me and I'm desperate for him.

Our tongues collide. A wicked dance of sensation and desires.

I'm lost, drugged. Intoxicated by this man.

Time stands still. It's irrelevant with his lips pressed to mine. I'm not sure how long we stay here. How long he makes love to me with his mouth, but with a strangled groan, he pulls away, and I cry out from the loss. Never wanting the kiss to end.

I gasp when his firm hands literally sweep me off my feet. "Where are you taking me?" I giggle.

"To bed."

Spencer walks us backward until my legs hit the bed and I'm pushed down. Lifting my eyes, I meet his gaze. The look reflected back is predatory. A caged beast ready to be let loose. He steps forward and then stops, his legs only a mere inch from where I lie. My breathing is erratic, my chest heaving.

He tugs his shirt off. His body is perfection. Tanned and toned. I want to touch him. I need to touch him. But he's too far away, and the look in his eyes tells me not to move. So I don't. I wait for him to take control.

"Take off your clothes," he orders.

The heat in his stare leaves no room for objections. I pull away my dress, leaving me in only my bra.

"Everything."

Slowly I remove the rest until I'm naked before him. His gaze rakes across my body.

"Perfect."

My cheeks blush, the embarrassment of my body on display rushing to my head. But the voices inside me telling me to cover are soon silenced by the pads of his fingers skimming my knees, pulling my legs apart.

"So perfect." He licks his lips. A hungry beast. "I need to taste you." His mouth presses to my skin and kisses a path up to my knees. I expect him to stop. To taste me where I'm so desperate to be touched. But instead, he continues up to my breasts.

"First here." His words blow on my skin like a seductive mist full of promise and mystery. My nipples pebble and peak at the sensation. The hot air caressing me makes my body come alive in a series of shivers. "Don't move," he says as he latches on, his teeth grazing the sensitive flesh.

There's a raw intensity to the way he devours me. His breathing is fast. My heart rate faster. Spencer moves one hand between my thighs, and a desperate whimper escapes as he pushes his fingers deep within me, but then withdraws them, leaving me hungry. Rotating my hips, I beg him to continue and he does, shoving two fingers inside me, pressing up until he finds the perfect sweet spot. The feel of them inside me causes sparks of heat. Static electricity. He pumps into me, over and over again, but just as I feel myself coming apart, he stops.

"Please," I beg, lifting my hips up to his hand, trying to force him back.

"On my tongue. I want to taste you."

He moves his mouth down the skin of my belly and

against my hip where he lavishes a soft kiss. Then he moves his body lower until his head aligns with my core and his mouth latches onto me. I thrash against the new feeling. Against the onslaught. My climax is so close. He licks and sucks as he presses me down into the mattress, his mouth and fingers working in tandem until I'm crying out.

Chasing the high.

Crashing over the edge.

Once I'm sated from my orgasm, he moves away and reaches for the table next to the bed. I hear the familiar sound of a packet ripping, and once sheathed he settles his body against mine. I widen my legs to give him access. Gripping his shaft, I guide him toward me, begging him to take me. He doesn't, though. Instead, he twists his hips in a seductive dance.

Teasing.

Torturing.

He settles deeper between my legs, making me believe that this is the moment. But it doesn't happen, his hard length resting upon my core.

"Please," I beg again.

Finally, he plunges into me with force. A primal moan pours out through his mouth, a desperate cry from mine. Once he's fully seated in me, I let out the breath I was holding. Feels too good. His body within mine is more potent than any drug.

He thrusts in slow strokes. In hard strokes. Long and

then slow. Our hips rotate together. He moves deeper into me and then withdraws.

He drives in and out, picking up speed. Thrusting at a punishing clip, his pace is maddening. I throw my head back, my eyes shutting as every muscle inside me clenches around him. Through my haze, I feel his body shudder as he follows me over the edge. Together we catch our breaths.

His weight is heavy on me as his breathing regulates and mine returns to its normal clip. A second later he pulls out. I want to beg him to stay, but I'm too tired. Too sated from the pleasure still coursing through every synapse of my body. My eyes flutter closed again and the most perfect, peaceful bliss engulfs me.

CHAPTER SIX

Olivia

THROUGH HEAVY EYELIDS, STREAKS OF LIGHT GLEAMS in. Blinking, they try to adjust to my surroundings.

Where am I?

The first thing I notice is the large plush bed I'm in, an unfamiliar bed and a very empty bed.

What the hell?

Where is he? Was it all a dream? The small ache of my muscles and the unfamiliar room tell me that last night did in fact happen.

Spencer Lancaster happened.

I look around for signs of him, but he's nowhere to be seen. In fact, the room is eerily silent. The only sound is coming from the soft drum of raindrops against the pane of the large floor-to-ceiling window across from the bed. The blinds are closed, thank God, or I'd worry that half of London had seen our previous night's activities. My cheeks heat at the thought.

I wonder where Spencer is?

With a stretch of my arms, I wring out all the sleep from my body and then get out of bed and tiptoe into the bathroom. Empty. I seize the opportunity to check my hair. *Catastrophe.* My hair is disheveled and my makeup smeared. Not a good look.

Turning on the faucet, I dampen a rag and wipe the black from my face, trying desperately to not rub my face red. *Better.* Then I run my hands through my hair to get the knots out and the hairs to lie down. When I'm done, the image I see is markedly better, but still shows signs of a late night romp.

I creep slowly and quietly into the kitchen, beginning to feel like an interloper. Again empty. I sigh in relief. I need a couple of minutes to compose myself before I come face-to-face with him. Last night was certainly not my first one-night stand, but there's something different this time. I actually want to know him. Even if he seems exactly like the media makes him out to be, a playboy. That alone is a reason for me to not care. For me to stay far away from him. But there was a moment when he held me in his arms when I was falling asleep that was tender. Not typical of asshole players. It's almost as if there's more to him than meets the eye.

I poke around the kitchen, desperately needing a drink of water, and that's when I see a note. I pluck it from the counter, discarding the single rose that accompanies it.

Beautiful,
I know this is corny and cliché but thanks for last night.

It was just what I needed. I'm sorry I had to leave early. Business calls. It's one of my last days here, and I need to tie up loose ends before I go to my next destination. Make yourself at home. I hope your stay in London is memorable.

I sigh at the last sentence. For once, my memories of London will be memorable. I won't ever forget our night together, but I can't help being a little disappointed. The next time I see Spencer Lancaster, it'll be on the cover of another magazine or tabloid.

I quickly collect my things, dress, and exit the room. When I check my phone, I have two missed calls from Lindsey. I should ignore them. I should get on the soonest flight out of here and back to the States.

Lindsey is my downfall. Almost every blackout bender I've ever had, I was with Lindsey. She's a party girl and with that comes drugs. I left her yesterday to avoid all of that. But being left behind by Spencer has me back to my insecure self. I knew it would only be one night, but still a part of me had hoped that he'd have said goodbye. A familiar feeling begins to creep into my blood, self-doubt, so I do the dumb thing. I open her message.

Lindsey: Hey, babe! Your stuff is still at my place, does that mean you're still in town!!?? What are you doing tonight? We're heading to Club X. Some major fun is going down.

Lindsey: Come join? Tabs on me . . . see you later xx.

What would one more night hurt?

Me: Where are you?

Lindsey: At the suite. Wanna go shopping?
Me: Absolutely!
Lindsey: YAY! My black card is burning a hole in my purse.

I roll my eyes at her incessant need to be so ostentatious. But these are the people I choose to associate with, so what does that say about me?

Me: I'll be there in 20.
Lindsey: Get ready to tie one on.
Lindsey: Tonight is going to be epic.

―――――――――――――◆―――――――――――――

The whole day Lindsey has me parading around town, going from boutique to boutique. I'm so tired by the end of it that I consider bailing on the rest of the night, but Lindsey wouldn't hear of it. Supposedly some billionaire socialite she's had her eyes on forever is in town and ready to spend a lot of money on expensive champagne. I haven't seen Lindsey this giddy over a guy in a long time, so I must admit my curiosity is piqued. She spent hours getting ready and is still fussing as we make our way into the club.

"I look horrible. My hair is a frizzy mess." Lindsey's voice shakes, her mouth tight. She reaches her hand up and tries desperately to flatten out her hair.

I've never seen her like this before. "Are you fidgeting?"

"I'm so nervous," she admits. She sounds stifled and unnatural, not the Lindsey I know.

I don't know how to take this side of Lindsey. The vulnerability is so real and entirely unlike her. For the first time, I'm seeing Lindsey in a different light. She appears to have it all, but the one thing Lindsey doesn't have is affection of any kind. Her parents are cold and uncaring. They give her unlimited funds to simply go away and leave them to their lives.

The truth hits me.

This whole time, Lindsey has been using alcohol and partying to mask her loneliness. She isn't unlike me at all. I see that now, and I'm ashamed that I've avoided and misjudged her. Perhaps we can help each other out of the dark.

I turn to Lindsey, knowing what she needs. "You look absolutely stunning. Any guy would be lucky to have your attention."

"Do you really mean that?" Her pinched brow and worry lines creasing her forehead tell me she doubts my words.

"I do. You are smart and gorgeous. You're a catch, and don't forget it."

Slowly a dimple appears on her cheeks. "Damn straight. Let's party."

It might not be what I wanted to hear, but that's Lindsey. It'll take more than one moment of solidarity to have her leaning on anyone. I mentally note that she and I need to actually talk more often.

We make it two feet before Lindsey is squealing. She's

clearly found her target. She motions across the room to a group of rowdy guys. One is standing on a table acting like the mayor. That has to be the guy Lindsey is fawning over.

She's out of her damn mind. He has to be half her age.

"Linds, how old is he?" I question.

"Does it matter?" she exclaims.

"Yes, yes, it does." My hands rest on my hips and I cock my head at her. "He doesn't look a day older than nineteen."

"He might not be. I'm not sure." She shrugs. She obviously doesn't care.

"You don't even know how old he is?"

With that, her mouth purses. "No, Olivia, I don't need to know how old he is. I only need to know that he's Pierce Lancaster of *the* Lancaster Hotel chains."

My head whips in her direction. "What did you say?"

"He's one of the Lancaster heirs," she squeals. "He has more money than all of us in this room combined."

"As in Spencer Lancaster's brother?"

"Duh! That's his oldest brother. Word has it he's in town too. I guess Pierce has been dodging him. So typical," she says offhandedly. "He's a bad boy, and I'm definitely going to tame him."

"Maybe the Lancaster boys don't want to be tamed."

"What's wrong with you?" Lindsey asks, cocking a brow at me.

"Nothing. I was just saying."

"Hmmm, all boys want to be tamed."

I scrunch my nose at her ridiculous claim. "He's too young."

"He's not that much younger than us," she whines.

"We're in our mid-twenties. If he's even twenty, I'd be surprised."

She shrugs. "Age isn't a big deal. Our families would be a perfect union. My father would be so proud."

The glint in Lindsey's eyes makes me sad for her. I don't even know if she really likes the idea of who Pierce Lancaster might be or she just likes the thought of his money and prestige. Even more concerning is the sudden realization that everything she's doing is to gain the respect of a man who doesn't deserve it. Her father ignores her. He's all but disowned her. She shouldn't be basing her decisions around what he'd want.

The night spins out of control quickly. Pierce proves to be a lot to handle. I can even see Lindsey's interest waning. He's a child acting more like a drunken frat boy than the heir to a one-billion-dollar hotel industry. He's turned Club X into Club XXX, taking shots between women's breasts and practically dry humping every waitress who will let him.

I can't help but think of the tabloids and what they say about Spencer. It's not too far off from the behavior I'm witnessing and that makes me sad. The Spencer I met was so different. I wonder what he would have to say about Pierce's behavior. Would he champion it?

There's a commotion to my left and I'm being pushed

out of the way by a couple of the guys Pierce came with. I stand on my tippy toes just in time to see Spencer Lancaster moving quickly in Pierce's direction.

This night just got a little more interesting.

CHAPTER SEVEN

Spencer

I NEED A FUCKING DRINK.

My brother doesn't know how to act respectable. I knew he was in town and he's been avoiding me, but when I got the call from the owner of the club telling me to come get my out of control hoodlum brother I saw red. I've had enough of his traveling the world spending all of his inheritance on alcohol, drugs, and women.

I don't know what his deal is, but we're going to get to the bottom of it when I'm back in the States. I drag him out of the club and put him right into a town car that's headed straight for a private jet to take him home. I'm not here to babysit.

Grant might not have anything to do with us, to do with the business, but that doesn't mean he gets to dump Pierce on me. It's time my other brother steps up and does something. It's fucking ridiculous.

I twirl the ice around my glass before taking a large swig. I need something to help me relax. I take another sip and look across the packed club. That's when I see her. The girl from last night. Our eyes lock, and I question whether I'm dreaming her. Her long, blond hair falls loosely over her shoulders, and her bright eyes stare at me as though she's seen a ghost.

I smirk at her reaction. I don't know her name, and I don't know why we keep meeting, but I'm damn glad we do. Last night was hands-down the best sex I've had in a long time and that's saying something. The fact that she didn't press me about who I was makes it even better. Anonymity is not something I have very often. I fully intend to bathe in it—and in her—as long as she'd let me.

Grabbing my drink, I stalk toward her, slow but purposeful. "Twice in two days. Am I a lucky bastard or what?" I flash her a dirty smirk.

"Sure are. Maybe you did something fabulous in a former life?" she deadpans dryly.

"Probably, because in this life I recall leaving you naked in my room. What are you doing here?"

The hazy gaze she wore moments ago is replaced by a mask of indifference. She doesn't fuck around. Not figuratively, anyway, and damn if it doesn't make her more attractive. "I'm here with friends. Are you here for a round two with a different blonde?" She's looking everywhere but at me, and if she's offended over my manwhoring ways, she sure as hell knows how to hide it. I move closer to her, my arm brushing hers.

"I had some business to deal with."

She lets out a harsh breath at my answer. "Business. Typical."

I can't help but chuckle. As hard as she's trying to act like she isn't upset about how I left, it's not working. I can tell by the straightness of her back that my leaving her this morning didn't win me any favors with her.

"I'm sorry, but that's why I'm here. I'm conducting business for my family."

She doesn't speak, so I continue.

"It was important, and I couldn't be late."

"So I gathered," she says, unimpressed.

"What's your name?" It's the worst thing I could ask, but I do it anyway.

She tilts her head to the side. "Thought we weren't sharing that information. Are you going soft on me, Mysterious Stranger?" Her eyes narrow with mischief.

My hands rise in defense. "You don't have to tell me. I can just call you beautiful." I grin.

She rolls her eyes. "Sounds corny, but I still prefer Olivia."

"Olivia." I test out the word. It rolls off my tongue sounding sexual yet beautiful at the same time. "I like it. It suits you."

She laughs, her ice-queen attitude melting a little. "I didn't choose it. My mother's quite fond of it, though."

"She has good taste. So, would you like a drink, *Olivia?*"

"I don't know if that's such a great idea." She lowers her head, seemingly embarrassed. "I'm about ready to head out, but I need to find my friend." She stands on her toes, looking around the room. I have to laugh. The place is packed. The likelihood of her finding her friend is slim to none right now.

"Who is he?" I ask, causing her to bristle at my words.

She snaps her head to me. "Excuse me?"

"You heard me, Olivia. Who is he?" The thought of her with some jackass has me seeing red.

"My friend is a girl. I don't make a habit of sleeping with different men on back to back nights." She crosses her arms, shooting daggers at me. "I do have some standards, thank you."

I've clearly pissed her off, but I'm relieved by her answer. "You're right, I'm sorry. Didn't mean to offend you, though you are particularly cute when you're red. Let me buy you a drink."

Her eyes narrow in disbelief. Did I just offer her cyanide? No. I'm pretty sure it was a drink. Yet Olivia is mighty feisty, and hell if it doesn't make her more appealing to me.

"As a truce," I add, nudging her shoulder with mine, because why not? Maybe that way she'll remember how fucking good it feels when our bodies connect, even through designer clothes and silky fabric.

She stays quiet for a couple of seconds, contemplating the offer, and finally nods in agreement.

"What's your poison?" I ask as we sit at the bar.

"I'd like a Stella, please," she says to the bartender.

"Beer?" I lift an eyebrow at her. *Interesting.*

"Yes. Beer."

I chuckle at her shortness. Every second I spend with this woman has me more intrigued. She's a complete conundrum, and I have the sudden urge to solve the puzzle that is Olivia. "What's your last name?"

"Do you really want to go there? If I tell you, you'll be forced to share too."

"Touché," I laugh. "So we're going to remain anonymous?"

"It's very film noir." She gives me a sidelong glance, under thick eyelashes and peppered with a mysterious smirk. "And therefore *so much* more fun. Don't you think?" I can't help but smirk at that.

"I do like your style." I order myself another whiskey.

"You should start by sharing your first name since you know mine."

"I think that's fair." I extend my hand to her. "Spencer. Nice to meet you."

She shakes my hand. At that moment, I hear a gasp behind us. I turn to see a girl, eyes wide.

"Liv, what . . . when . . . how?" The friend stutters nervously.

I know she knows who I am, and I've got to stop her before she outs me in front of Olivia. I like that she doesn't know who I am. She doesn't act differently around me. I raise my hand to the intruder.

"Hello, I'm Spencer." I put that out there, hoping that quells her curiosity enough.

"Lindsey, there you are," Olivia states.

Lindsey looks at me with cold eyes. "Someone forced Pierce to leave, and now I'm bored and want to go home."

Her whiny voice annoys me immediately. I stay silent, hoping that somehow I come out of this talk unscathed.

"Yeah, I saw that," Olivia says, looking at me.

I stiffen. *Does she know?*

She turns her head before I can gauge what she saw. "Do you want me to leave with you?" she asks her friend.

Lindsey looks back and forth between Olivia and me. "No, I think you should stay put. I'll catch a ride with Murph. Call you tomorrow." She smiles devilishly as though she knows something we don't. Without another word, the girl turns on her heel and practically skips off.

"I thought you were leaving today." Olivia's voice draws my attention her way.

"I was until I got a call that I needed to be here."

She squints. "Your business is at Club X?"

"No, but something came up and I had to be here to meet with someone."

She looks around. "Looks like you've been stood up."

My body sags in relief. She clearly didn't see me with Pierce or she'd know what my business here was. "Nah, I already took care of it."

She nods. "So . . . about last night," she says hesitantly, her voice shaking slightly.

"Daydreaming about me?" I tease, loving the way her cheeks stain a dark shade of pink. It would look even better on the cheeks under her panties. Though it's probably best if I don't mention it right now.

"No. Yes . . . I mean, what?"

Her confusion is cute, and I typically fucking hate cute. My type is more like the stewardess on my jet. Bold and overtly sexy. Olivia's beauty isn't contrived. She's natural and definitely not arrogant.

"I had a great night with you, Olivia. I didn't want it to end." It's the truth. I did enjoy our time together.

"Me too." Her voice is low. The words come out with a sweet innocence that makes me hyper aware of how much I crave a second round with her. That in itself should serve as alarm bells, but I choose not to listen. "I'll admit I was a bit disappointed when you were gone this morning."

"Do you want to get out of here?" I know it's a ballsy move, especially after ditching her this morning, but I suddenly don't want to be here anymore. It's only a matter of time before someone else recognizes me, and I'd like to just have a little bit more time with her. "I know things weren't supposed to go past last night, but I really enjoyed my time with you and I'd like to hang out more, but not here."

She taps her mouth with her finger. I expect her to say no, but she doesn't. She stands and extends her hand to me. I take it and move us toward one more night of fun and freedom.

CHAPTER EIGHT

Olivia

WHEN WE GET OUTSIDE OF THE BACK OF CLUB X to avoid the paparazzi, Spencer turns to me. "This night is almost as fucking gorgeous as you are. We're walking."

"Bossy, but I'll take it." My lips part into a huge smile. I can think of nothing more perfect than walking with this man.

The fresh air breezes through my hair, sheltering me from his penetrating stare, and I melt on the spot when he grabs my hand, holding it in his. We walk, taking in the sights and just enjoying the night, not needing to say anything to fill the space.

"Sorry about leaving this morning," Spencer says, breaking the silence.

"You had work to do. I understand that." I did. I understood working hard. The need to be successful. The hunger he felt . . . I felt it too. The hole in need of feeling . . . I had it too. In my mind. In my heart. *In my stomach.*

"I did, but I want you to know how hard it was to leave."

I turn to him, narrowing my eyes. "You barely know me. It couldn't have been too hard."

He smirks at my words, a small dimple forming in his cheek. He looks devastatingly handsome. The small dimple makes me melt. Was it always there? How have I missed it?

"True, but it was."

Small butterflies start to swarm in my belly at his words and I squeeze his hand, silently thanking him for them. "I'll admit I was a bit disappointed."

"Yeah?"

"Yes." I laugh. "I wanted to say goodbye."

"You didn't want to get my number?" He raises a brow.

"No, I don't need it. I'm not under any illusion that this is going to be something more. I just wanted to kiss you one last time." I drop my head in embarrassment at my admission.

Spencer stops us, turning me to him. Without saying a word, he drops my hand and brings it up to my head, cupping my cheeks in his hands. His thumb caresses my skin, sending more butterflies flying in my abdomen. Our eyes pierce each other's, and he finally leans down, capturing my mouth. I sigh into his kiss, feeling light-headed and blissful. His mouth is tender yet firm. It's the best kiss I've ever had and I never want to leave this moment. Here we are in London under twinkling lights, with no cares in the world at this very minute.

"Olivia," he breathes my name into my neck. A silent invitation in his tone.

"Yes."

———————————

The rest of the walk back is a complete blur. Each street we pass, each piece of exquisite architecture is lost on me. I'm completely consumed by the feel of his hand against the small of my back. The presence of his body next to mine. The small circles his fingers caress into the silk of my dress. I can barely speak. All I can think about is feeling his lips again, the way his mouth tastes . . .

Over and over again everything from the previous night plays in my head. Like a record on repeat, one I hope will never end.

We're barely inside the door before he pounces. He pushes me against the wall, my back hitting the hard surface causing the air to escape my lungs. It doesn't hurt, though. It's exactly what I need. His desperation is thrilling. Better than any drink or drug.

His arms wrap around me and in one quick pull, our skins touch. He begins to grab at my waist, pulling us even closer, fusing us together while he captures my mouth. His kiss is long and passionate. Hungry and promising.

It tells of desire and need.

He doesn't stop kissing me as both of his hands work to undress me. He pulls the straps away from my shoulders and down my arms until it falls in a heap on the floor. My breasts are free and I stand completely naked against his body, my bare skin rubbing against his clothes.

His pupils dilate.

"Fuck," he growls as his gaze scans my body. His hand reaches out, my breasts large and full in his hands. He pulls at each nipple. "This whole time. The whole walk . . ." he grits out, pulling and kneading on the sensitive skin. "You were naked under your clothes. Do you ever wear underwear, Olivia? Or are you always ready?"

"Panty lines," I pant back. Not able to say more. I'm too lost in the intensity of his touch on my bare skin.

"I could have fucked you anywhere. Did you want that? Were you ready for me?" He pulls his hand away and skims down my body, finding me hot and ready for him. "Fuck, you were." His fingers part me. "Is that what you wanted? Did you want me to fuck you? Do you want me to fuck you now?"

"God, yes," I moan against his chest as he thrusts a finger inside me.

"So wet. So ready."

He picks up the pace of his ministrations. My chest begins to heave and I let out a sharp intake of breath as he bends down and places the tip of my breast into his mouth sucking and latching hard onto my nipple. A moan escapes my mouth as he continues licking and thrusting at the same time. The two sensations overwhelm me, setting me ablaze.

I'm on fire.

Every inch of me ready to combust.

"I want to feast on you," he mutters, his head still buried against the skin of my chest. "And then I want to fuck you against the wall. And when I'm done, I want to fuck you on every other surface of this room. Tell me you want that?"

"Yes," I whimper, my head thrown back in the throes of passion. My body starts to tighten around his fingers.

"No." He halts his movements, and I whimper a protest. "I want to feel you come apart around me."

He pulls his hand away, and I can hear him reach into his back pocket. My eyes watch with desperation as he pulls a condom out. His movements are hurried as he rips it open, sheathing himself. "Fuck," he groans as he presses all the way to the hilt inside of me. "Too good. You feel too good." He pulls out and then thrusts back in.

"God, yes. Right there," I pant, drunk on him, drunk and high off the feeling of him inside me again. My words fuel him as he picks up his pace. Fucking me harder. Deeper. The penetration and angle are too much. My body begins to quiver and quake, and as it tightens around him, he burrows his head in my shoulder, biting down on my skin as he trembles inside me.

We stay up against the wall for a minute, allowing us to come down from our high. My legs shake uncontrollably as I try to regulate my breathing. He kisses the skin on my neck, and then out of nowhere, brackets his arms around me and throws me over his shoulder.

"I'm not done with you." He steps away from the wall. "I never did get a taste." We head straight toward the bed.

"Stay," he orders, throwing me down as he leaves me on the bed and goes to the bathroom to discard the condom. He returns with a hunger in his eyes that spreads a chill up my body. Without preamble, Spencer spreads my legs apart and crawls on the bed. He angles his body between them and kisses his way up my leg. Closing my eyes, I wait.

His breath grazes me.

I squirm under his perusal.

"Patience." His tongue darts out and licks me so lightly I fear I might have imagined it. I buck, my hips lifting to demand more. "Shhh. I got you," he coos and I whimper as I wait. It feels like forever, the thud of my heart counting the seconds until he gives me what I need. What I'm so desperate for.

With slow, steady moves, he swipes his tongue along my slit from bottom to top. It's perfection. Utter perfection the feel of his mouth on me.

"You taste delicious. Like the sweetest fucking dessert I've ever had." Spencer continues his assault on my senses. It's too much and not nearly enough. I need him inside me again.

"Inside me," I beg. "Please."

Pulling away, he looks down at me and I look up at him through hooded lids. My vision drops as I see him fist himself in his hand and start pulling himself from root to tip. While I watch him touch himself, he thrusts his fingers inside me until I'm primed for the taking. After two more thrusts of his fingers, he pulls away and reaches for a condom, the whole time still fisting himself. He rolls the condom on and with his free hand, he spreads my legs farther apart, crawling up my body and placing himself at my entrance. I bite my lip in anticipation and then with one quick thrust of his hips, he's fully seated.

His movements pause, allowing me to adjust to the sudden invasion. Once I am, he pulls out and then he slams back in. Then pulls out again and slams back in. Spencer keeps up that pace. Dragging in and out.

Over and over again.

At first he's slow, but as my nails wrack the skin of his back he begins to fuck me harder. He pulls out again, but this time he doesn't thrust back in. Instead, he hovers over me, leaving me vacant until I moan with need. His own breath comes out in ragged spurts. The anticipation of his next thrust drives us both insane. When I think neither one of us can take another minute of this sweet torture, he starts the pattern all over again, and again, and again.

In and out.

In and out.

The sounds of the headboard banging against the wall, of our bodies moving together and our breathing has me falling over the edge. Blurred vision, hammering heart, everything inside of me shudders.

"Fuck . . ." he screams into the skin of my neck as his body tenses and then releases.

We lie in bed next to each other, sated and spent of energy. Sex with Spencer is like nothing I've experienced before. He's passionate, generous, and most of all . . . skilled.

"What's going through that pretty head of yours?" Spencer asks, drawing me into his side possessively. Not in a way a lover would, but an owner. I like this. With him, I like feeling small.

"Nothing," I lie, not wanting to ruin the moment. I only want to bask in it for as long as I can before this perfect dream fades away and I have to return to reality.

"You seem to have the weight of the world on your shoulders."

I turn my head toward him. "Very perceptive of you. But what about you?" I ask, trying hard to change the subject.

"What do you mean?" He feigns ignorance, but the twitch in his cheek gives him away.

"Tonight. You came stalking into the club and you didn't look happy." I pause, contemplating my next words. "What happened?"

He rakes his hand through his unruly hair and sighs. "Family business."

"That's vague."

"My brother. He's fucking up left and right and I just happened to be in the same city as him this time. Something needed to be done."

"Yeah, Pierce was out of control tonight," I say before I can stop myself.

Spencer stiffens next to me. *Shit.* "You know my brother?" he frowns. His tone doesn't give away his feelings. I can't tell if he's upset about the revelation.

"I just met him tonight."

"You know who I am then." It isn't a question, so I don't answer.

"I've known since the first night who you were," I say in a neutral voice. It's true. No reason to lie.

"Why didn't you say anything?" The furrow on his brow shows his concern.

"I didn't find it important." I shrug. "We were keeping things no strings, and so I thought it didn't need to be discussed."

"You didn't try to find me after I left you."

"Why would I? We didn't even exchange names that first night."

"But you knew who I was."

"And?"

At this, he rolls me on top of him so we are face-to-face. "I'm a very wealthy man, Olivia."

I scrunch my nose in distaste. "So? Why the hell does that matter?"

"You don't care?"

"No, not really," I say, trying to get off him, but he just pulls me closer to him.

"I like how easy this is."

"I like you. I have fun with you. Why should it matter how much money you have?"

"Wow. You're something else, Olivia."

I raise my brow in challenge. "And what might that be?"

"Different."

The sincerity in his eyes melts all the tension away, replaced by want. I don't care if this is just for one more day. I'll take it. He makes me feel special, and that's something I haven't felt in a long time. Every second I spend with Spencer Lancaster I come dangerously close to falling head first in love with him. I thank my lucky stars that he's leaving London soon. It's what's best, because if this continued and ended badly, I don't think I'd survive it.

"I'm not different." If I were different, it wouldn't have been so easy for him to have left me that first night. Even now, it's only a matter of time before he goes.

He narrows his eyes. "Are you doing that girl thing where you disagree just so I'll tell you again?"

I chuckle. "No. I don't need you to say anything to me. This is sex, Spencer."

Small lines form on his brow. "It might be sex, but I'm serious, Olivia. You are different and you're gorgeous too."

I smile.

"That smile is your best feature. You should do it more often."

I smack his chest. "I do smile."

He flips me over so he's on top. "Since we have the

smile down, let's work on some other things."

"Like?"

He leans down, kissing me hungrily. I know where this is going, and I'm happy to work on that all night if he'll allow. He groans after a few minutes and pulls away.

"As much as I'd like to stay up all night fucking you, I have a lot of work to do tomorrow."

"Oh. Okay."

"What do you have going on for the next two weeks?" Spencer asks.

"Nothing. I was considering heading home to the States, but there isn't anything pressing." *Other than my funds drying up and having to dip into my savings or worse, needing to crawl back to my parents for money.*

"I have to head to Marseille this week and Barcelona the week after that. I'm looking at properties to potentially develop Lancaster Hotels on."

My teeth bite down on my lower lip, my heart breaking just a bit knowing our time is ending.

"Would you like to accompany me?"

I stop breathing for a second. Wondering if I heard him right. "What?" I scrunch my nose in confusion.

"Travel with me," he clarifies.

"Wouldn't that be a bit much?"

"I'm not asking you to marry me." He chuckles. "I just thought that while I'm still in Europe, and you're still in Europe, perhaps we could tour Europe together." He shrugs.

I search his face and find nothing. "Just Europe?" I narrow my eyes.

"Just Europe." He grins.

"Let's do it."

CHAPTER NINE

Olivia

THE SUN POURS OVER ME IN BRILLIANT ORANGES AND reds, skating across the distance and into the horizon. I bask in it, lounging on a chaise on our private villa balcony at Château Saint-Martin in Vence, France. My view is incredible, stretching out to the waters of the French Riviera. Breathing in the air, it's easy to marvel at this life. I've enjoyed many luxuries, but none this extravagant. This is a vacation from my life. I have no current job prospects and soon will be broke. A part of me feels like Julia Roberts in *Pretty Woman.*

And suddenly, the parallels have my stomach plummeting.

You're no better than a prostitute.

I'm here knowing there's no chance of a future with Spencer, yet I enjoy all the trappings that come with two weeks with him. I wonder if he's drawn the parallels. Does he view me in such a way? My insecurities gnaw on my fragile psyche. The last thing I want to be to Spencer is hired entertainment. *He's not paying you. But does he really want to be with you?*

No one really wants to be with you.

My phone chimes and I look down to see it's him.

Spencer: I'm finishing up business now, but I have plans for us tonight. I'm taking you on a date.

My heart swells at the word date. All my insecurities from moments ago melt away to the fact that he used the one word I needed to hear. *Date.* Escorts aren't taken on dates. They're taken to business events.

Me: I'd love that. What time should I be ready?

Spencer: I wanted to do a little touring of Vence. It's cool. I think you'll really enjoy it. Two hours work?

Me: Perfect.

My phone vibrates again a second later and I think it's going to be Spencer texting again, but instead, I'm met with the name Bridget on the screen.

"Hey, sis."

"Hey, yourself." Her voice crackles and echoes through my ear. We must not have a good connection. "Where are you?" Bridget asks.

"The strangest thing happened. But I can't really get into all the details right now."

"Vague much?" She laughs.

"I don't want to jinx it." Being with Spencer is my little secret right now and I don't want anyone spoiling it for me.

"Well, that sounds interesting." Her voice raises an octave.

"I hope so," I sigh.

"Can you at least tell me where you are? Our phone connection is shit. It's obvious you're far away."

"That's another thing I'm in Vence." I move to sit up in my lounge chair.

"Vence? Where the heck is Vence?"

"Umm, it's in France," I mumble and I'm not sure she can hear me because the line is completely quiet for a beat before I hear her sharp intake of breath.

"Shut the fuck up!" *Oh, she heard me.* "God I'm so jealous of you right now. Are you with a guy?" *Only Bridget.* Her mind always jumps to boys. Or in my case men.

"What's there to be jealous of?"

"You get to travel the world. It's so glamorous what you do." If she only knew how unglamorous my life really is. This trip with Spencer is completely out of my norm.

"Don't be jealous. Being a model can suck sometimes. Trust me." I take a deep breath. "Plus, you still have plenty of time you can do anything. You can travel."

"I'm sure as soon as I graduate Mom and Dad are going to be on my case to get a job."

"Have you thought about what you want to do?"

"No," she deadpans.

"You only have a few more months."

"Don't remind me," she whines, and I laugh. "So when are you back in town?"

"A few weeks."

"Maybe I'll come in right before my summer finals."

"I can't believe you had to do summer session in order to graduate," I tease.

"Har har har. Really funny. When I'm back in town, you won't be laughing."

"Ha. Sounds like a good plan. Listen, I have to go. Call me if you come in."

"Will do. Love you, sis."

"Love you too."

"One more thing, send Mom and Dad a text telling them you're okay. They're worried about you."

"On it."

After I hang up the phone, I shoot them a text letting them know I'm in France for work. Even though I shouldn't lie, I don't want to tell them where I am. It's not that I'm embarrassed but I also don't need to answer all the questions that will surely arise if I tell them I'm on vacation with Spencer Lancaster. Once I get that out of the way, I lean back in my lounge chair and get comfy.

It will only take me an hour to get ready, so that gives me an hour to just enjoy this view and relax. I'm not sure when I'll be able to take a vacation like this again, I might as well enjoy the free time. I pull up the Kindle app on my phone and begin to read some fantasy story that takes me away from my real world worries, placing me in a fictional character's life for just a while. It's full of villains and heroes, princes and princesses, damsels in distress. I don't feel like a damsel at this particular moment, but I envision Spencer storming in on a white horse to rescue me from my perils and I can't help but sigh. My over imagination has always been an issue.

That's not real life, and I'd be best to remember that so my heart isn't crushed when Spencer and I part ways in two short weeks. I push that thought down, intent on enjoying the rest of my day.

Two hours later, I'm dressed in a white, shift dress with a scalloped neckline, hair pulled low on my neck in an intricate braided bun. I've no idea where he's taking me, and I hope I'm not underdressed.

At the exact time he said he'd be here, Spencer comes strolling through the door looking amazing. My breath hitches. "Hi." My words come out soft and measured, trying to control the nerves that cause my face to flush as my eyes freeze on his full lips.

"Hi." His masculine voice does odd things to my body, making me warm and dizzy. "You look fantastic," he says as he strolls toward me. He places his hand on my cheek in an intimate gesture. "You're making it hard for me to leave these walls."

"Yeah?" I say, having nothing better to comment with.

"But I promised you a date and a date you shall have." He takes my hand and pulls me into him, placing a small kiss on my lips. "Give me ten minutes to clean up and we'll go." I watch as he moves toward the bedroom, and I can't

AVA HARRISON

help but want to follow him.

———————•————————

Excitement courses through me as I take in our surroundings. The town of Vence reminds me of an adorable medieval village straight out of a children's book. The market is robust with colors and people, and the town feels alive with excitement. It has the feeling of a daydream, one where you could easily get lost in the sights and smells surrounding you. Here I'm not Olivia, and he's certainly not Spencer Lancaster. We're just two people getting lost in a fairy tale.

"Do you like it?" Spencer asks, stepping up behind me. "It's amazing, right?" His mouth tickles the nape of my neck, and I turn my chin to give him greater access. The warmth from his lips teases me as he speaks. It makes my heart pound erratically like it might burst out from behind my ribs. God, I want him. It's not natural how much. It's only been a few hours since he's touched me, and I feel desperate for him to find a small alcove and ravish me.

As if he can hear my thoughts, his arm snakes around my waist, and I press my hips back into him. A groan escapes his mouth. Before I can think, he spins me around and nips at my lower lip, but as fast as he kissed me, he's pulling away and grabbing my hand. With one squeeze, he motions to go deeper into the village.

Hand in hand, we maneuver our way through the

78

cobblestoned streets, through endless little alleyways, up and down the narrow paths. We pass through the market, spotting quaint shops and little restaurants. When I see a small souvenir shop, I make him stop so I can peek inside.

"What are you looking for?" Spencer asks as I'm searching every nook and cranny of the store.

"A snow globe, " I say over my shoulder, not bothering to look at him.

"A snow globe?"

"Yeah, I collect them. Always have. Every location I've been to."

"Really? Why?"

I turn at his question. "It's a tradition I've had with my family since I was little. I don't know when I started, but it's been a constant in my life. Something I can always depend on. No matter who goes away or where they go, I get a snow globe. There's something magical about a snow globe. It's perfect and then you shake it. Chaos. It's magnificent chaos. You almost don't expect it to settle, to go back to normal. You know what I mean?"

His stare penetrates mine. "I do," he mumbles, and I wonder what he's thinking.

"When it does settle, nothing has changed. It's just as perfect as when it started." Turning back around, I lift on a tiptoe, but I'm too short.

"Here, let me."

I move out of the way, and Spencer steps forward. When he turns back around he's holding two snow globes with the medieval town of Vence captured inside it.

"You have two?"

"I want to start the tradition." He smirks, and a part of me melts at the gesture.

After Spencer pays for the globes, we walk back into the winding street. "I thought we could stop and have a drink before dinner." He points to a building behind me.

From the outside, the restaurant is weathered and worn. Old stones and brown storm shutters greet us. The ivy that crawls up the side of the building only adds to the perfect ambiance.

"This place is spectacular."

"The restaurant is an old mill. Would you like to grab a drink there?" he asks.

"I'd love one." My cheeks burn from the smile spreading on them. I can't remember the last time I've been this happy.

Spencer leads me up the stairs and over to an empty table on the patio overlooking the square. Just as we sit, an older woman approaches our table. She carries two menus in her weathered hands.

"*Que puis-je faire pour vous?*"

"*Deux verres de rosé, s'il vous plait,*" Spencer responds, leaving me floored. His accent is perfect. Lord does he sound sexy. She nods and walks away, leaving us alone to sit in a comfortable silence until she returns.

"You speak French?" I whisper in awe and turned on all at the same time. I can feel heat spread against my cheeks and the way he's looking at me, it's obvious I'm flushed and he knows the reason why. His eyes twinkle in mischief before he speaks.

"I do. And it seems you like it when I do. I'll need to remember that later tonight." He winks, and my face grows warm at the thought.

A few minutes later, she returns with a newly opened bottle of rosé, and with perfect precision despite her years, she pours us each a glass and leaves.

With my knees crossed, I lean forward and grab my drink. "Thanks for taking me here. It's stunning."

"It is," he states, but he doesn't say more. Just stares at me with heat in his eyes.

"Have you ever been to Vence before?" I feel a bit flustered by the way he's staring at me.

"This is a first for me, but the location is unlike anything I've ever seen. It would make for a perfect addition to my portfolio of properties. Have you ever been to France?" He leans back in his chair, still scrutinizing me with his crystal green eyes.

"I've been to France for a few runway shows, but never been to this area either."

"And do you like it, Olivia? Have you enjoyed your stay in Vence?" He smirks at me. His gaze is wicked with innuendo.

"I do. And you? Are you enjoying yourself?"

"Immensely."

"I'm happy to hear that. I like hearing what you like.

You know, it's funny. We've spent all this time together, and yet I feel like I don't know anything about you."

His brow lifts, but I can see a slight tic in the jaw.

"No. No." I raise my hand up. "Nothing personal." I roll my eyes.

He laughs, and his lip tugs up into a smile.

"Simple stuff."

"Simple stuff?"

"Yeah, you know, like your favorite color?" I laugh but then stop when he answers.

"Blue."

"Oh, okay. I was joking with that question, but I guess since you shared, I guess mine is . . ." I think for a second and our gazes catch. "Green." The word tumbles out of my mouth before I can stop it. *Shit.* I hope he doesn't make the connection. His smirk is evident against the stubble of his jaw. I can feel heat spread across my cheeks.

"Favorite food?" I say quickly to pull the attention away from my embarrassing revelation, but with the way he studies me, and the gleam of his white teeth through his grin, my cheeks are officially on fire. "*Real* food," I huff, exasperated by the direction the conversation is going.

"You are real." He winks.

"You're too much . . ." I laugh, and he joins in with me, lightening the mood and the sexual energy that has been coursing through the air.

CHAPTER TEN

Spencer

'VE GOT TO BE LOSING MY FUCKING MIND. I DON'T KNOW
what came over me when I asked Olivia to join me for
the next two weeks. I just knew I didn't want things
to end so soon with her. If I could have two more weeks
then fuck it, I was going to take it. We both know how
this is going to end, so if she's okay with extending it
then who am I to question things? That might make me a
selfish bastard, but I don't care.

We've been all over Vence since finishing our cock-
tails. Strolling through the markets and seeing some of
the biggest tourist sights like the Tower of Saint-Lambert
and the Cathedral of the Nativity of Saint Mary. Watching
Olivia's eyes wide with amazement has been an experi-
ence I'll never forget. It's not often that the women who
accompany me are actually in awe of things. I tend to sur-
round myself with women who want for nothing. Spoiled,
entitled, bitchy women. Anything and everything they
have access to. It's so hard to please a woman who has

everything, and it's interesting to find Olivia is not one of them.

It occurs to me that I know nothing about her. We chose it that way, but typically I can ascertain a few details regardless of how badly I'm trying not to. The only thing I can gather about her is that she's not from a wealthy family. Well, that's not entirely true, but her family isn't my type of wealth. The *Lancaster* type of money.

"How long have you been a model?" I blurt out.

Olivia turns to me, looking weary. "I'm not modeling anymore," she says curtly and starts moving away from me.

I pull her back, unwilling to let her get off that easily. I didn't become the CEO of Lancaster Hotels by giving in. "What happened to that?"

"Do we really want to ruin the day by talking about this? I thought we had agreed to keep things anonymous. Simple questions only. Remember?" Her tone is clipped.

"We did." I nod. "I just want to know you a little better. Is that so bad?"

She chews her lip. "Let's just say I no longer have the look that the photographer was going for and my agent then fired me."

I scrunch my brow, not getting her meaning. "What? Why?"

She sighs. "Apparently everyone thinks I'm overweight."

My jaw slacks in disbelief. "Are you fucking kidding

me?" I say angrily. "You are anything but overweight, Olivia." I spin her around toward me. "I think you need to speak to an attorney because that has to be illegal."

"It's just not worth it. It's his word against mine."

I pull her in close. "We may not know much about each other, Olivia, but I'll tell you this right now," I pause to collect my temper "you're one of the most captivating women I've ever met, and don't let anyone tell you differently. If you love modeling, pursue it. He may not see what he has in front of him, but someone else will."

She smiles. "Thank you. I needed to hear that. But in all honesty, I didn't love modeling. It was an opportunity that came at the right time." She steps away, lowering her head and picking at her nails. "While I was in college, a lot of stuff went down at home, and I really didn't want to go back there." She shrugs. "When the modeling contract came up, it was the perfect excuse to get as far away from home as possible. Plus, the money was great." She looks at me finally. "I took it and ran. I don't regret it, but I don't want to go back. I need to find something else to do."

"Can I help?" I offer without even thinking. I can't give her a job with Lancaster, but I can call in some favors. It's the least I could do.

"No. I'll be okay, but thanks." She takes my hand in her own and squeezes. We walk hand in hand down the street, taking in the sights and letting the tense conversation of moments ago slip away.

We walk for a while longer just enjoying the scenery.

My view is fucking fantastic as I take her in. She's wearing a tight little dress that's about mid-thigh and shows off her tan skin, which looks edible. Her hair is pulled up so you can see her neck, and instantly I want to be anywhere but here. The need to have her alone is intense, but I promised her a date.

"Are you hungry?" I ask.

She gives me a sidelong glance, and I watch as her cheek tips up into a knowing grin. "Depends on what you're asking." She chuckles. "Food can wait, though. I have a feeling you're wanting something else."

I flash a sinister smirk. "I didn't say anything."

"You didn't have to. It's written all over your face."

"Is that so?" I quirk my brow.

"You're a man after all."

"I'll show you a man," I growl, picking her up and throwing her over my shoulder in the middle of a crowded street in France.

She squeals. "Put me down, Spencer," she commands, embarrassed, but I don't care who's watching. Right now it's just me and Olivia. Everyone and everything melts away. I sound like a fucking girl, but I mean it. This is the most fun I've had with a woman . . . ever.

"Okay," I concede. Sliding her down my chest, I stop her so we're nose to nose. "Kiss me," I demand and she doesn't hesitate. The mint on her breath does something to my already low self-control, and I swear to God, I fucking growl.

"If it's any consolation, I want it just as bad as you," she whispers for my ears only.

I grunt. "Doubtful."

She giggles, sliding the rest of the way down.

This woman will be the death of me.

CHAPTER ELEVEN

Olivia

TODAY WAS EXTRAORDINARY. EVERYTHING FROM THE sites we visited to the conversation was beyond my expectation. There's so much more to Spencer Lancaster. The tabloids have it all wrong. He's the type of man who takes your breath away. The type of man you lose your heart to. I need to keep my guard up because that outcome is not in my favor. He won't return my feelings. I'm not the type of girl Spencer ends up with.

Not perfect enough. I have too many flaws.

Now I sit across from him at L'Ambroisie. The cuisine is to die for, and I moan around a mouthful of ravioli.

"You like?" He stifles a laugh.

"It's so good." I beam.

"You were hungry."

I grin. "Starved."

A waiter approaches our table and Spencer rattles off something in perfect French. The way it rolls off his tongue you'd think it was his native language. It's so sexy. I know a little Spanish, but that's the extent of my language scope. Our worlds are so different, and in this moment it's obvious. But I refuse to spoil the mood, so instead, once the man has left, I focus on Spencer.

"What did you say?"

"He asked if we wanted dessert and I passed. I hope that's all right. I should've asked you."

"I'm completely stuffed, so you made the right choice." I smile. "So since you broke the rules before, how about you tell me something about yourself, Spencer. Something a little deeper than your favorite color or food."

He sits back without saying a word. Any laughter that had previously danced in his eyes evaporates, replaced with a stone-like stare that is void of emotion. Several seconds go by, and I can't take the awkward silence. "I just assumed since I shared something personal earlier you could return the favor."

"I'm very guarded, Olivia." He places his napkin on the table and looks into my eyes. "Do you know how many times I've been with a woman only to find that she ran off to the first tabloid she could find?" The mention of him with other women doesn't sit well with me, but I let it go, instead focusing on everything else he said. "Nothing I say ever stays in confidence."

"I can't imagine. I'm sorry, Spencer," I say sincerely. "But I'm not like those girls. I wouldn't ever break your trust."

"You say that, but when things end in two weeks you

might not feel the same," he huffs.

"Do you intend to treat me badly?"

"No, but, we'll go our separate ways soon and maybe you won't be happy about that when the time comes."

I bristle. "You have a very high opinion of yourself," I scoff, angry at his insinuation that I'll want more but he won't. "I'll be perfectly fine parting ways with you when the time comes. I'm not looking for any more than you are." I move to stand.

"Olivia, wait," he says. "I didn't mean to offend you. I was just trying to point out that in the past, these types of arrangements didn't end well for me."

I cringe at the word *arrangement*. "Arrangement? You make me sound like a call girl," I spit.

"No, I didn't mean it like that. Stop putting words in my mouth."

"Stop being an ass."

"All I'm saying is girls in the past have developed feelings beyond what I did and they didn't take it well." He sighs. "I didn't mean to compare you to them. I'm sorry."

I sit. "I'm sorry I overreacted. I just don't like to be compared to other people. When I agreed to this, I knew what I was getting into. I'm more than fine with this *arrangement*."

Spencer cringes when I throw that word back in his face. "Okay, now I see why you don't like that word."

I purse my lips. "Can you just tell me how your meetings went this morning?" I try to steer us away from this conversation. He lets out an audible sigh and his shoulders noticeably drop in relief.

"I found a piece of property I think would be perfect for a hotel. Right now I just have to wait to see if my price is accepted."

"And if it's not?"

"Then we start negotiations. Very seldom does the first offer get accepted. I'm sure there will be some haggling involved."

"And so you're going to do the same thing in Barcelona?" I quiz.

"Yes. I'm looking at another piece of property, hoping to take the name international. It's the next wave of securing the hotel line."

"Why hasn't it been done yet?"

"My father started Lancaster Holdings, Inc. It was a large undertaking to make it what it is. We are one of the largest privately held companies in America. I guess he was so busy building an empire in the United States that he just never saw a reason to go international."

"What changed?"

"My father and I are very different. He's old school, set in his ways. I'm always looking toward the future. Trying to find ways that we can grow, how Lancaster Holding's can adapt to a forever-changing environment. First thing I announced when I was made CEO was expansion." He shrugs.

"How did your dad feel about that?"

"At first he didn't take it well. But at the end of the day, I think he was relieved that he had retired and it was no longer his responsibility. His only responsibility was to spend more time with my mom."

"Do they have a good relationship?" I probe, loving the view into the life of Spencer.

"They do. They have what you could call a fairy-tale relationship."

The thought of that type of marriage makes me smile. One day I hope to have that too. "What was it like growing up with two brothers?"

"There's a big age gap with Pierce, so it was always Grant and me," he says. "Did you know we're only twelve months apart?"

"I didn't."

"Yeah, we're practically twins. It was always us. Together. Playing. Horsing around. We were the best of friends. When Pierce was born, Grant and I used to hide for hours from our parents but especially from the nanny."

"Didn't like the new baby?" I probe.

"Oh God no, we hated him." With that, he laughs. "As Grant and I got older, we were still close even though we went to different schools. Grant decided to stay in New York and work for our father in his free time. I traveled the world. Studied architecture. Learned from books and life. He busted his ass. By the time he graduated he knew all the ins and outs while I was off doing God knows what."

"Learning. You were off learning. You just had a different teacher."

With that, he looks me in the eye, and he knows I understand. "Yes, exactly. I was learning all about building infrastructures. I was never supposed to be the boss."

"So what happened? Why didn't Grant take over?"

"He chose a different path."

"And what was that?"

"He chose love." There's an edginess to his voice I can't understand. "So, Olivia, what about your family?"

And here we go turning the tide back to me and a topic I'd rather avoid. I want to push forward and demand more information from him, but I decide not to spook him after he finally let me in and that it will be better if I reciprocate and tread slowly where he's concerned.

"My parents love each other. It hasn't always been easy between the two of them, but they work really hard at it. There was a time they were separated and my father was with someone else." I inhale, not wanting to discuss that time.

His lips pinch together as he thinks of what to say.

"Oh? How did that go?" he finally asks.

"About as you can expect."

"Your mom forgave him?" He crosses his arms across his chest as his forehead creases.

"She did, but it hasn't been easy. We just found out recently that his time with the other woman resulted in a child." I watch his eyes widen in disbelief.

"Shit. Are you okay?" he questions, and my shoulders lift.

"I am now. My half-sister is great."

He nods, listening intently.

"I was in college at the time, so I wasn't around when shit hit the fan, but it was really hard on my younger sister because our half-sister is actually her best friend."

His eyes widen. "What? How the hell?"

"It's a sordid story, but it boils down to my dad didn't have a clue about her. The woman withheld that and apparently as large as New York is, it's actually a small city. My sisters went to private school together."

"Is that why you took the modeling job?"

"It's part of it. Things just spiraled out of control from there." I don't offer any more, and thankfully he doesn't pry.

"I know all about family issues."

I raise a brow. "I've heard rumors, but I don't put much stock into what the tabloids say."

He smiles. "Thank God."

I smirk. "I'm sure if I read half of the shit they put out there about you, we wouldn't be sitting here tonight together."

"I'm wounded," he teases.

"You should be," I joke.

His mouth twitches and eventually curves up into a smile, but it's the look in his eyes that turns my insides to mush. They're intense. They make silent promises to me.

Promises I can't wait to receive.

I slip off my sandal and slide my toes up his leg. I hear his intake of breath and smile at the reaction. "We should get out of here," I say breathily.

"Please," he groans.

I slip my shoe back on and stand, holding out my hand. He takes it, pulling me into him for a kiss. "I can't wait to get you out of this dress," he says into my neck.

Red creeps up my neck, coloring my cheeks. The heat is almost unbearable. I don't know how I'll make it on the walk back.

We step into the room. My movements halt when Spencer's footsteps stop. Turning around, I look at him. His face is stern, his eyes smolder. I move toward him, but he lifts his hand in the air to stop me.

"Take your clothes off," he commands. His voice is husky. Heat spreads in my lower abdomen at the way his gaze penetrates me. It's as if he's already undressing me.

Slowly, I strip off my clothes and stand naked before him. My eyes are looking down at the floor.

"Look at me." His stare is penetrating. "On the bed."

Lying on my back, my body quivers as I wait. The anticipation of his touch is almost too much for me to bear. His eyes sweep the length of me, but he doesn't move. He doesn't touch me. I groan.

"Touch me," I beg.

Spencer's head shakes at my demand. He takes a step closer. "Patience." Now at the foot of the bed, his finger touches the skin of my ankle as he pulls my legs apart. "I want it slow. I want to savor you. I want to lick and touch every inch of your body. I want you screaming and thrashing under me." He sits on the bed between my spread legs. "And then and only then will I give you what you want."

The soft touch of his mouth moves against my inner thigh as his lips begin to trail up my leg. He crawls all the way up my body, planting kisses until his tongue swipes against my breast, capturing my erect nipple into his mouth. The sensation is too much.

Intoxicating.

Heady.

I want more. Need more.

Spencer answers my silent desires. His hand skims down, settling between my thighs. I buck at the contact.

He chuckles.

"Is this what you wanted, Olivia?" My name on his tongue sounds like a seduction. But I don't need a seduction; I'm already desperate for him.

His hands continue to explore, parting my swollen flesh and sliding inside. I gasp, panting heavily as his fingers pump in and out of me. When he pushes his digits up, my inner walls clench around him. My head thrashes back and forth as I reach my climax.

After my orgasm ceases, Spencer doesn't stop his

ministrations. Instead, he stokes the fire, setting me ablaze. Through hooded lids, I watch as he removes his hand from me and licks his finger in his mouth. Once it's all clean, he undresses, grabs a condom from beside the bed and then crawls up my body, teasing my entrance with his hard length. Gripping his shaft, I guide him to where I want him.

He inches himself in then retracts. I want to scream. I want to pull him into me. His eyes meet mine, full of mischief. With one strong thrust, he pushes in and out of my body. Ragged bursts escape. My nails scratch at his shoulders as I brace for each push and pull of his body. He slams in over and over again, moving his hips at a faster clip until I'm flying over the edge.

CHAPTER TWELVE

Olivia

THREE DAYS HAVE PASSED SINCE WE WENT TO VENCE. *Three glorious days.* Spencer spends the days working while I enjoy the beautiful property. I can't remember the last time I've been able to unwind like this. To not have anything to think about other than just being happy. But it's bittersweet as I know our time together will end soon.

Shaking off the thoughts, I head back inside from the balcony and sit down next to Spencer on the couch. He has files in front of him as he listens to someone speak on the phone. He doesn't look at me, but his hand lifts and lays on my forearm, the pads of his fingers making circles on my skin.

"Okay, find out for me," he says before putting the phone away. "So what do you want to do today?"

I turn my head and look up at him. "Are you speaking to me?"

"Who else would I be speaking to, Olivia?" He has

the most delicious smirk I have ever seen and I just stare at him loving the way his eyes watch me. "So what do you want to do today?" he repeats pulling me from my thoughts.

"Wow, Mr. Lancaster. You're letting me choose? How very gracious of you." He shuts me up by placing his mouth on mine and I laugh into his lips.

"I let you choose all the time. Everyone else, no. I call the shots," he responds as he pulls away from me.

"Can't always be the boss."

He chuckles at that. "Oh no, Olivia, I'll always be the boss." His voice is husky, his gaze dancing over my skin and making me feel all warm and tingly inside. "So what's it going to be?"

"How far are we from Provence?" I joke, knowing it's too far for us to go when he has so much work to do.

"Is that what you want to do?" He starts to fiddle with his phone.

"You have to work," I reply. Secretly hoping and praying that he doesn't.

"I don't *have* to do anything today. Only what I want. And today, I *want* to go to Provence with you." He stands up and walks out of the room.

An hour later I'm dressed and standing at a heliport in Nice.

"I can't believe you rented us a helicopter."

"You said you wanted to go to Provence, so come on. Let me help you up."

He helps me in and buckles me up. Once we're both seated in the back, he reaches out and takes my hand in his. Our fingers entwine, his lip pulls up into a relaxed smile. It's a smile I've never seen on him before, the way it cracks his face makes him look younger, peaceful.

Through beautiful scenery we hold hands, and I watch as we pass over quaint towns on our journey. When we land, I'm even more shocked to see a driver and car waiting for us. And not just any car. It's a Mercedes Maybach.

"Bonjour, Mr. Lancaster, *je suis François. Je serai votre chauffeur pour la journée. Voici le colis que vous avez demandé.* " I have no idea what the driver says to Spencer, but he hands Spencer a small nondescript brown bag before opening the back door for us.

Stepping into the back seat of the Maybach, we begin the short drive to the vineyard Spencer has arranged for us to tour. We drive through tiny roads that weave in and out of lavender fields. Purple stretches into the horizon. It's like a dream.

When we arrive at the family run vineyard near the village of Sault, we're greeted by a handsome older man. He looks to be in his early sixties, salt and pepper hair surrounding his tanned and weathered face. He shows us to a rustic rough iron table set in the midst of sprawling hills, and in the far distance, mountains loom. The sun beats down on us, and the air is thick with the scent of flowers. The man walks away and when he returns he places a series of flight glasses in front of us, I smile at all the wine that we are going to be tasting.

"This is perfect."

"I knew you'd like it."

"Like it? I love it. Rosé is my favorite. I can't wait to taste all of these."

He lifts his chin. "Noted."

For the next hour, we sit and sip the wines. We talk of nothing important but everything. He makes me laugh. Makes me smile. He listens to me intently, as if he finds me interesting, as if I'm more than my profession, more than my face. He can see past the walls of perfection I hide behind. It's unnerving and exhilarating all at the same time.

When I put down my most recent glass, I see Spencer staring at me intently.

"I bought something for you," he says.

"You didn't have to buy me anything."

"I didn't have to, but I wanted to."

"When?"

"I have my ways." He winks. Reaching into the bag the driver gave him, he pulls out a tiny snow globe.

"For your collection."

It might be small, but the gesture makes my heart race.

The next morning, I wake once again to an empty bed. This has become an everyday occurrence since I've known Spencer Lancaster, but this time I hear Spencer's voice as it carries through the villa.

"That's fantastic news. Thank you for getting back to me. I'll have the money wired by the end of today."

I try to pretend like I'm sleeping as Spencer comes waltzing in. I don't want him to think I was eavesdropping.

"Get up, woman. We have some celebrating to do," he says excitedly.

"Is that so?" I say, popping upright. "To what do I owe this pleasant mood?"

"They accepted my offer, and we can close the deal by the end of today. We'll be able to break ground this coming spring."

"That's wonderful news. Congratulations, Spencer." I beam.

"I like to think it's because of my good luck charm." He winks, moving toward me.

"I'm pretty lucky," I smirk.

"Of that, I'm sure, Olivia." He leans in to kiss me. "Would you like to come and see the property with me?"

"You want to show me the property?" I say, shocked.

"Don't freak, Olivia. I'm not asking you to buy a house, just to see a piece of land." He grins.

"Good thing because if you were, I'd be running."

He chuckles.

"Sure, I'll come. It would be great to see a day in the life of Spencer Lancaster."

"It's pretty boring."

"I doubt that," I quip.

"It's been much more exciting lately," he says as he pulls me in close.

"Yeah?"

"Definitely." He places a small kiss on my lips. "Get dressed. We leave in an hour."

The view is breathtaking. I have no doubt a lovely building will sit on the sand some day. It makes me a little sad. It's such an exclusive piece of property, hidden from the rest of Antibes. It's a shame that a massive hotel will be placed on top of it, making it no longer so private.

"What's on your mind?" Spencer asks from my side.

"This piece of land is so beautiful and a hotel will take away from that."

Small lines start to crease Spencer's forehead.

"It's just so peaceful here like its own little slice of heaven. You build a hotel, people will come, and it will no longer be quiet."

"Then what, my dear Olivia, would you put on this property?"

I think for a moment before answering. "Nothing. It would just be my own little paradise to come and sit and watch the waves lap."

"You're quite the romantic."

"Because I have a lack of it in my life." The words slip out before I can stop them. And I hope it doesn't make the moment awkward, but when I hear him chuckle, I let out the air I didn't even realize I'm holding.

"Something tells me it won't always be like that for you, Olivia."

"I don't know." I shrug. "I'm not in any rush. When he comes along, I'll know it. He just hasn't shown up yet."

He turns his head as if done with the conversation.

It's a little awkward talking to him about my future with someone else, but there's no future for us. And in this moment, I get a little pang of sadness at that realization.

"I take it back," I say to change the subject.

He turns his head toward me.

"I think I'd put a private residence right here. I wouldn't want to just come here occasionally. I'd want to wake up to this view."

He smiles. "I can see you here."

We walk hand in hand down the shoreline, taking in the magnificent waters that stretch out in front of us. The French Riviera is something to behold. I'm sad that this is my first time ever being here. I vow to myself to come back here one day.

"Are you ready to move on to Barcelona?"

My head turns to him quickly. "We still have a few more days here."

"But I sealed the deal. There's no reason to stay here any longer. The sooner I get to Barcelona, the sooner I can start those negotiations, and hopefully, can be on a plane back home."

That familiar ache returns when I remember what Spencer and I are doing together. He isn't just enjoying his time here with me. It's all business, and I'm just along for the ride. A part of me grows sad at the thought, but he did warn me not to get caught up with ideas that wouldn't happen, and I have no one to blame but myself. I've gotten wrapped up in the beauty of everything surrounding me that I forgot my place in his life. This reminder will stick with me.

I won't make the same mistake again.

CHAPTER THIRTEEN

Olivia

S PENCER HAS CALLED IN FOR HIS FAMILY PLANE AGAIN, but this time it's to transport us from Nice to Barcelona. I must admit I'm not a member of the mile-high club, and the thought of embarking on that journey with Spencer sends shivers down my spine in anticipation. Last time I was on the plane I was so nervous it hadn't crossed my mind, but this time it infiltrates my every thought. We're boarded and waiting for the crew to get prepared when a sultry voice comes over the speaker. I feel Spencer tense next to me, and I eye him with curiosity.

"You okay?"

"I'm fine," he says curtly.

"Are you a nervous flyer?"

He scoffs. "I fly all the time. I'm perfectly fine in the air."

"Okaaayyy," I mutter.

I'm about to open up my Kindle and start some reading when a busty brunette comes around the corner and shoots daggers directly at me. *She wasn't on our last flight.* "Who's that?" I say under my breath.

"No one I know," he replies, but his body language suggests otherwise. He clearly knows this person.

She approaches. "Spencer," she croons. "How are you?"

I arch a brow at her. What the hell? Is she really coming onto him in front of me?

"My name is Mr. Lancaster, and you'll do well to remember that," he says icily.

Her face instantly falls into a pout. "But—"

He cuts her off. "We haven't even left the ground. I can have you replaced in two seconds if you speak to me again."

She goes stiff. "Is there anything I can get you?" she says tightly.

"Two glasses of champagne, please."

Her eyes go wide and she looks murderous before stomping away.

"What was that all about?"

"I can assure you, Olivia, you don't want to know."

My stomachs sours. Clearly this is just one more girl in the long line of Spencer Lancaster conquests. I wouldn't be surprised if his sordid details end up on the front page of the *Expositor* by tomorrow given her expression.

"Nice," I say, my voice flat.

"Olivia, what happened in the past should stay there. Let's not ruin our last few days together by focusing on things that have nothing to do with the two of us."

"I don't care what you've done in your past. I just don't like to be lied to."

He sighs. "I'm sorry I lied to you. I just didn't want to start a fight. I had no idea that she'd be on this flight."

"Perhaps, moving forward, you shouldn't sleep with your staff," I suggest coldly.

"I'll take that advice."

The girl returns with our drinks, handing them over roughly. As she turns to walk away, Spencer calls out. "Victoria."

She turns to him.

"Please don't interrupt us the rest of the flight. We'll be heading to the bedroom."

She snarls and returns to the pit.

"Was that necessary?"

"What?" he feigns innocence.

"We're heading to the bedroom?" I wrinkle my nose in disgust.

"I thought you'd like to sleep on the way."

"I'm sure that's not what you were trying to insinuate."

"I'd never use you as a pawn, Olivia." He grabs my hand, kissing my palm. "I'm not that much of an asshole, at least not to you."

I can't stop the swelling of my heart at that. He might not say it, but it's obvious he cares. *About me.* I'm suddenly feeling playful, so I lean over and whisper, "So . . . about the sleeping . . ."

His brow quirks. "You want to sleep?"

I smirk. "Nope."

"What exactly do you have in mind, Olivia?"

"I'm missing a very distinctive membership that can only be achieved by being miles high in the air."

He chuckles at my lame explanation. "Is that so? We can't have that."

I shake my head. "No, I agree."

He stands and holds out his hand. "Let me officially usher you into a club that will change you forever." His gorgeous dimple makes an appearance, and I swoon. Hard. Little does he know just how much he's changing me forever.

I may never recover.

CHAPTER FOURTEEN

Olivia

SURE ENOUGH, THE NEXT DAY VICTORIA IS OUT OF A job and Spencer's face is plastered all over the tabloids. Headlines read Spencer Lancaster flies high with mystery woman. The article goes on to detail all the sordid details of Spencer and Victoria's time in the air and then flashes to his latest rendezvous with a mystery woman. I'm nauseous reading it, but it's nothing I didn't already suspect. I just feel bad because it's exactly what Spencer had said. Nothing in his life stays secret, and he can't trust anyone.

Now our first day in Barcelona is spent with Spencer doing damage control with his publicist. Neither one of us wants people to know that we're together, especially since it ends in less than seven days.

"Are you fucking kidding me?" I hear Spencer yell from the other room. "I want her ruined. Those details couldn't have come from anyone but her." Huffing ensues followed by more tense words. "No, Clarissa, absolutely not. There's no way that Marshall would've known that. He was busy flying the fucking plane, and he knows better. He's been with our family for years." He lets out a growl. "I want her buried along with this story. Take care of it now or find yourself another job. There are plenty of people who would be clamoring over themselves to work for me."

I busy myself by taking out my Kindle and pretending I'm reading, not wanting him to know I overheard all of that.

He comes stomping in. "This is a fucking shit show."

My stomach falls. "What?" I can tell by his face what he's about to say isn't good.

"I can't believe the bitch told the press about us. But that's not the worst part."

My mouth slacks. I knew it was a horrible idea I should've said no to. But honestly, I couldn't resist him. "What is the worst part?" I whisper, scared of what he will say.

"All of the tabloids know about it and have their dogs out looking to find out who this mystery mile high girl is."

I cringe. If I didn't already feel like a prostitute, this just cements the deal.

"I'm sorry," he says sincerely.

I can tell this whole thing is eating at him.

"We're going to have to lay low in Barcelona," he says solemnly. "If you want to go home, I can understand. I can arrange for Marshall to take you back."

The thought of leaving him has me feeling even worse. I'd rather hide for a few more days and enjoy my time with him at night. I'm not ready to let go of our time.

"No," I say sheepishly.

"Good." He smiles and then begins pacing. "I never wanted to throw you into my fucking issues." He stops right in front of me, taking my face in his hands. "I'm so sorry, Olivia."

My forehead scrunches. "Why are you apologizing to me?" I ask.

"I'm the one who put you in their line of fire. Between my fuck up with Victoria, and then my display on the plane, it was all my fault."

"Stop. I'm a grown woman. I made choices too."

"Choosing to spend your time with me is a mistake, Olivia."

"No." I shake my head. "My time with you has been everything." Again words slip out of my mouth that I know I shouldn't be saying to him. But for some reason, he makes me lose all reason. A part of me is nervous about my revelation. That he might reject me, or remind me of what this is, but instead, Spencer devours me with his mouth. Our tongues tangle in passion and anger. For him, I can imagine it's anger at Victoria, anger at himself. For me, it's anger because I'm falling against all the warnings. I should do the smart thing and tell him I changed my mind. I should get on that plane and never look back. Forget London, forget Vence, and most importantly, forget I ever met Spencer Lancaster.

But I can't. I don't want to.

My anger fuels me to kiss him harder. I want him to remember these lips. I want my memory to burn him at night when I'm gone. This isn't making love or even having sex. This is desperation.

He picks me up and I wrap my legs around his waist. Carrying me to the bed, Spencer never pulls his lips from mine. We fall into a heap on top of the feather mattress, roughly removing each other's clothes. Panties are tossed, bra is flung, and once it's all discarded, I watch through hooded lids as he rips open a condom wrapper and sheaths himself. Once he's finished, I lower myself on top of him, sighing at the absolute relief I feel. He follows with a moan of his own. We never slow in our movements. It's fast and hard, but we move in synchronicity.

In this position, we're eye to eye. There's something disarming about being this vulnerable side to him, but I want him to see just how much he affects me. He holds my hips, helping me to glide up and down. Our eyes lock and I see it. He may never admit it, but in this moment I know he feels the way I do.

I throw my head back and bask in the exquisite feel of him inside of me and the knowledge that I'm not alone in these feelings. He soon follows me over the edge and we lie in our contentment.

CHAPTER FIFTEEN

Spencer

THE NEXT MORNING, I WAKE OLIVIA UP EARLY TO TAKE her out for coffee before I have to work. The tiny café I want to take her to is tucked away in a small alcove amongst the vibrant city architecture. This city. These lines. When I'm here, I almost want to abandon my post as CEO and just design. I let out a breath. It would certainly be easier if I could. Then there would be none of this bullshit with the tabloids.

The fucking *Exposé* article is everywhere. I know Olivia must have read it by now, but we haven't discussed it. We should. But I'd prefer just to pretend it didn't happen. But that wouldn't be fair to her.

As we step inside, I place my hand on her back and guide her in. A small empty table lies in the corner. I guide her there, and once she's sitting, I head over to order us some coffee.

"*Dos cafés con leche y azúcar por favor.*" My Spanish isn't as good as my French, but it's still passable.

After our order comes, I sit beside her. She smiles at me. A smile that is so bewitching it knocks the air out of my lungs.

"You speak Spanish too?" Her eyes are wide with surprise.

"Not well," I mutter out.

"I heard you. If I didn't know better, I would think you were from here. Is there anything you can't do? Any language you can't speak?"

"That was one of the things my father insisted upon my brothers and me. Well. Who knows about Pierce."

"How much older are you than him. I saw him, he looks like a baby next to you."

"I'm thirty-two," I say, and I can't believe this is the first time we are talking about this. "Grant is thirty-one. And Pierce is the baby at twenty-two."

"Big age difference there."

"From what I was told, they tried for a year after Grant but couldn't get pregnant, my mom always wanted three kids. Nine years after Grant, they got themselves what mom likes to call her oops miracle. It's why he's so damn spoiled. Since the day he was born, he's been given everything he's wanted with out having to work for shit."

"Did you have to work?" she asks, and her eyes widen at the way her words left her mouth. "I didn't mean it like that." She bites her lower lip, and I look at her, and something pulls inside me. Not liking to see her unsure or nervous.

"I have always had to work. My father was much harder on Grant and me. It's almost like he gave up on Pierce. Too old or something."

"And now? With Pierce."

"My father is a good man, but he has no patience for him. It's probably why he ends up on every tabloid. He's probably seeking attention."

"You never know. Pierce might not be seeking attention as much as he's seeking approval. When I first started modeling it was because of my boyfriend in college. He's a photographer. The first time he took pictures, he told me I was beautiful. But then the backhanded comments started. Suddenly, I wasn't skinny enough, pretty enough. But I had already known the feeling of his approval and I needed that so badly I found myself doing things I'd never do to try to win his approval back."

I stare at her for a moment. Not knowing how to form the words to describe how amazing. I think she is. How strong I think she is. I understand the need for approval, I have felt the pressure every day of my life.

"I understand the need for approval. And although you might be correct about Pierce, at the same time some of his antics are solely for attention."

She gives me a once over. "Are any of yours?"

"I'm not like the man they describe, Olivia. Sure I have made some bad choices. Yes. Recently I made some fucking bad choices, but regardless. In the position I am in life, I'll end up there. Front and center. This is my life. There is nothing I can do about it, but it's not yours." Her face pales at my words, but I keep going. "I like you, Olivia, but this won't change. I need to know you can handle it. I won't be upset if—"

"I can handle it," she says full of conviction, and it makes me stop for a second.

She's breathtaking.

Her understanding. Her compassion. And then on top of that, she just takes me for what I am. She doesn't want anything from me. She gets me.

She's not pushing me to open up, but I realize that's exactly what I want to do. I want to open up. To her. To this. As I lift my coffee to my mouth, I realize my reservations about keeping my distance from Olivia are gone.

CHAPTER SIXTEEN

Olivia

After coffee and breakfast, we spent the day lying by the pool, or at least I did. Spencer was still doing damage control. After he was done with work, we took a bath together and experienced just how much fun that can be. Now, the daytime has faded into night. After a few minutes of just lying in his arms, a feeling of restfulness weaves its way through me. I'm enjoying this too much. Enjoying him. But I can't get used to this. This will end. The room grows warm, claustrophobic. *I need air.* I extract myself from his grip to throw on a silk robe.

"Where are you going?" he asks from the bed.

"Out on the balcony. I want to look at the stars." It sounds like a plausible excuse. I don't want him to know I'm getting panicky over my feelings for him.

He smiles. "I'll join you."

I nod and wait for him to throw on a pair of sweat pants. Once done, he walks up to me and trails his hand down my arm until he encases my hand in his.

We walk out into the dark, night stars shining on us from above. He sits in a lounger, grasping me around the waist to sit on top of him.

"You smell so good," he says, running his nose up my neck and placing a kiss below my ear.

I shudder at the touch. "I smell like you." I laugh.

"Yes, you do. I like that."

At that moment, fireworks explode overhead as if we're in the middle of a movie. There's a festival of some sort happening in the streets not far from our villa. You can hear the people cheer at the display.

"This is a perfect night."

"Mmm-hmmm," he groans into my neck.

"Thank you for bringing me here."

His grip tightens around my waist. "I wouldn't want anyone else to be here with me."

I turn my head to look at him. "Do you mean that?"

"Of course. I would never lie to you, Olivia."

I sigh. "It's just putting ideas into my head and it's not good."

He turns me the rest of the way so I'm straddling him. "What type of ideas?"

I mewl. "You know exactly what kind of ideas. This is ending in a couple of days. We both agreed that was what's to happen. I agreed, Spencer, and now . . ."

"Go on," he prompts.

"Now I'm not sure if that's what I want." I hang my

head, embarrassed at my admission.

He brings his hand below my chin, raising it so that our eyes meet once more. "You're right. You weren't supposed to want that. We agreed."

I nod, wanting to cry but refusing to allow my body to betray me so greatly.

"But things change, Olivia. I haven't met a woman in a long time who I wanted to see again. Who I wanted to spend time with."

My heart stops.

Breathe in. Breathe out.

I will myself to replay his last words to assure myself I heard him correctly.

"What are you saying, Spencer?"

"I'm not done with you"—he motions between the two of us—"with this." I wait for him to say not yet. Because eventually, he will be done but I don't say that. Instead, I ask him to clarify before I get my hopes up.

My brow rises. "You're going to have to explain to me now."

"I want to see you when we get back to the States."

"Meaning?" I press, needing him to confirm. I won't let him off easy. He needs to say the words.

He chuckles. "I want to try, Olivia." He smiles. "I want to get to know you, and for you to get to know me."

I kiss him. Hard.

After several minutes we break apart. "I've never wanted something like this before," he admits. "It scares the fuck out of me."

"Me too." I smile. "You came out of nowhere and just kinda stuck on me."

He laughs. "So I'm a leech?"

Now it's my turn to laugh.

"I suppose a very good-looking leech."

"Now there isn't any reason to hole you up in this room. That's as long as you're all right with the media finding out about us."

I smile. "I couldn't care less about them."

"Let's get some sleep so we can see Barcelona tomorrow."

I sleep soundly in his arms. Knowing that we have a possible future puts me at ease and on cloud nine.

"Holy hell," I mutter out. My eyes are stretching wide to take in the sight before me. "This is fantastic."

"It is pretty amazing." I look over at Spencer. He's appraising the magnificent building, but not in the same way I am. He's looking at it with respect, with precision.

"I love coming here. Seeing this inspires me. I look at the lines. The details. I imagine my buildings, my designs stretching out into the horizon."

"I don't even know what that's like. To see something like this and be inspired . . . I don't have that."

Spencer looks down at me, his chest rising and falling

slowly. His eyes are narrow with concern.

"Isn't there something that you feel passionately for?"

My stomach feels like it will bottom out. Is there anything I've ever felt passion for? "Honestly. I don't know." When the shit hit the fan in college, about my dad having an affair and fathering another kid, I dropped out and then I went off to model. I was so distracted partying I didn't think of anything else. When my grades slipped, it was just easier to give up. Modeling fit right in with my life at the time. It never even dawned on me to do anything else.

The rough pads of Spencer's hands lift my chin up. "What's going on in that gorgeous head of yours?"

"I-I don't know . . ." I admit on a sigh. "I never thought about it." I don't say anything else. What would I say? I allowed my family life to mess with my future. I let myself get completely lost until I almost hit rock bottom and lost everything. I can't say that, so instead I shake my head and plaster the biggest smile on my face. I do what I'd been programmed to do—smile big to the camera, show my best profile, look pretty—only with Spencer, it is hard to be plastic. He peeled the layer I put on when I face the world, and he deserves more than this. More than the fake-me. "I fucked up in college," I admit on a sigh. "With everything with my family . . ." My hands run through my hair as I try to explain what I'm trying to say. "I used it as an excuse to not try. I took the easy way out and started modeling rather than figure out what I really wanted from life." It's quiet for a minute. Neither of us speaks, but Spencer must sense my desire to not talk about it anymore because he pulls me toward him. "Come on. I want to show you the view from the top."

Once at the top of the building, my words are lost in my throat as I come face-to-face with nature at its most unique, with concrete art meeting urban superiority.

This moment. With Spencer. There are no words. With the city around us, the sun beating down on me. My hand encased in his.

This moment is the beginning of something special. I can feel it. By the way he squeezes my hand he can feel it too. There's air in my lungs, but I can't seem to get rid of it or breathe deeper. I feel alive—so raw and perfect—I want to take this moment and place it in a bell jar. I want to remember it. The scent of his aftershave—bitter on my lips and sweet on my skin. His strong features as he stares at the view in the eye like he defies it. I don't even mind that his attention is divided between the stunning land-scape and me.

Because it's not. Not really.

We're one in this moment. An entity that has no begin-ning, middle or end.

We blend together; we mesh and create something beautiful and different.

We're in a snow globe that belongs only to us, and I don't dare shake it.

For once in my life, I want it to stay still and quiet. No

flakes. No storm. No nothing.

Just Spencer and me.

Just when happiness meets life.

The next several days are magical.

With no end looming in sight, we can just relax and enjoy our time together. We see all of the famous sights of Barcelona and then some. We window shop and even find the most perfect snow globe to always remind me of my time here.

Now I'm bone tired, so I head back to the villa while Spencer goes to scope out the property. At some point I must have fallen asleep because I'm awoken by soft kisses being trailed up my neck.

"Do you have a love affair going on with my neck?" I tease.

"Mmm-hmmm," he murmurs softly.

"How was the property?"

"It was great. I don't like it as much as I did Antibes, but it will do nicely for a hotel."

"There's no better property than the one in Antibes," I say wistfully.

"Get up. I'm taking you to dinner."

"Do I have to move?"

"Yes. Take as much time as you want to get ready and then we'll leave."

"Do you have reservations?"

"I don't need reservations."

I turn to look at him, eyes widened in mock surprise at his ego. "Why, Mr. Lancaster, you have quite a sense of self-importance."

"Guess it comes with actually being important," he deadpans dryly.

"Well then, by all means, show me just how important you are."

"I'll show you how important I am," he says, rolling me on top of him.

I can't help but giggle at his playfulness. "If we start this up, we'll never get out the door."

"True story."

"Although dinner is sounding better by the minute."

He throws a pouty face my way, looking all sorts of adorable.

"Take me out on the Barcelona town. It's not every day we're in a beautiful country." I stand and rush to take a shower. When I emerge from the bathroom, a garment bag is lying across the bed. I narrow my eyes at the thing. Where did it come from? I call out for Spencer, but I don't receive a reply. In true Spencer form, there's a note lying next to the bag.

Olivia,

I purchased this earlier today. I'm sure you'll look gorgeous in it. Go ahead and get ready, and when you're done, come meet me in the lobby bar.

Spencer

I smile at his thoughtfulness. Who knew someone so opposed to relationships could be so good at one? I unzip the bag and gasp at the beauty of it. It's a knee-length black cocktail dress. As I inspect it further, I find it has a slit clear up the side, making it sexy.

I slide it over my body, and it fits like a glove. I look into the mirror and have to smile at the elegance of it. Mr. Lancaster sure does have amazing taste.

I can't wait for him to see me in this.

I finally make it down to the lobby bar, and stop short when I see a stunning woman leaning in toward Spencer. My back goes straight, and I have the sudden urge to vomit. I watch as the strange woman laughs at something Spencer says. His back is stiff, and he's not smiling, which helps to ease my worry, but the bottom line is, he hasn't moved away from her.

All the stories about Spencer and his playboy ways play through my mind like a bad movie. Now that we're together, will he stay faithful? I have to mentally smack myself. This is a new relationship, and I need to trust him. He's done nothing to give me reasons to doubt him, so I have to believe he's just being friendly.

I straighten my back and walk with confidence toward my boyfriend and the woman who's stealing his attention.

When he sees me, a slow, sexy smile breaks out across his face. The woman notices his gaze and follows it to me. Her face falls when she sees me. I internally smirk.

Spencer stands and makes his way toward me, not even glancing back at the woman. When he reaches me, he takes me in his arms and kisses me. "You look beautiful."

"Thank you," I breathe.

"They have a table ready for us."

I incline my head, looking toward the woman once more.

"Don't worry about her. She's no one. Just someone I'm doing business with."

I purse my lips. "She clearly is *somebody*." My words drip with disdain, and I have to will myself to rein it in. The last thing I want to do is sound like an insecure, jealous girlfriend. "I'm sorry. Let's enjoy our evening." I smile up at him, hoping he agrees to drop it. His return smile is answer enough. He takes my hand in his and leads me toward the back of the restaurant where they have set up a private table. "It's beautiful," I say in awe.

White candles illuminate the plush navy tablecloth, and a large chandelier hangs above giving the private room a soft glow. I notice that two places are set with elegant place settings and a bottle of expensive champagne. My shoulders uncoil from my previous bout of jealousy. *He really went all out.*

Spencer pulls out the chair for me to sit. Soon a waiter is tableside, ready to pop the champagne. Spencer dismisses him shortly after he shares the specials so we can decide on our meals.

"This is amazing. Thank you, Spencer."

"I'm happy you're here with me. Besides, we have much to celebrate."

I raise a brow. "Do tell."

"We agreed on a price for the Barcelona property. Paperwork should be drawn up shortly."

"That's wonderful. Congratulations, Spencer." I clap my hands, truly excited.

"It's a great deal. I'm very pleased."

Dinner is wonderful. We celebrate, eat, and eventually fall into easy conversation. We're holding hands, discussing plans for when we get back to New York when Spencer's phone begins to vibrate. He pulls his hand away from me and checks the name on the screen. Small lines start to mar his perfect face and every muscle in his body seems to tense.

"Everything all right?" I ask, concerned.

"Yeah, it's just—"

His words are cut off by a commotion in the next room. The next thing we know, people are swarming into our room, cameras drawn and snapping picture after picture. Questions are being hurled our way so fast I can't even process what's happening.

"What the fuck is going on?" Spencer's voice booms loud over the uproar.

"Mr. Lancaster, did you know your mystery woman is

Olivia Miller?"

He narrows his eyes. "I'm well aware of who my girl-friend is. What's the meaning of all of this?" he bellows, irritated.

"Did you know she's a recovering coke addict?"

Spencer flinches.

"That she's best known for passing out on the runway?"

"I think you have your facts mixed up. You all need to leave now before I call the authorities."

"Mr. Lancaster, aren't you embarrassed to be slum-ming it?"

He stands abruptly, ready to pummel someone. I jump to my feet, trying to stop him. "Spencer. Wait."

The manager comes running in. "I'm so sorry, Mr. Lancaster. These rats got past our hostess. I've called the authorities." I go to Spencer's side, grabbing his hand, pulling him away from the photographers.

"I'm so sorry I didn't tell you," I mumble out looking down at the floor in shame.

"I need a few minutes, Olivia. Let me help get the ass-holes out of here, and I'll be back, okay?"

I nod. Spencer and the manager usher the photogra-phers out of the room, and I'm left alone.

Spencer and I have talked about a lot of things these two past weeks, but my sordid past wasn't one of them. I didn't want him to know that I'm a recovering addict. He's so strong and professional, and I'm pathetic and weak.

I didn't want him to see that about me so soon. It's too soon.

I sit at the table, waiting for Spencer. I wait and wait . . .

But he doesn't return.

CHAPTER SEVENTEEN

Spencer

WHEN THE LOBBY MANAGER, AND I FINALLY GET these fucking pricks out of the bar, I step out back for some fresh air. I'm devastated that Olivia had to be ambushed like that. I know she's a model, but I'm sure she's not used to the paparazzi harassing her at dinner.

The words the assholes threw at me come back to mind. *Recovering coke addict.* Olivia said her past was bad, but a coke addiction? We clearly have a lot to talk about.

I start my way back to her when my phone begins buzzing in my pocket. I look down to see it's Grant, again. My brother and I haven't spoken in forever. If he's calling me something has to be wrong. I click accept and hold my breath.

"Hello?"

"Spencer." Grant's voice is strained.

"What's wrong?"

"You need to come home. It's Dad." The fact that Grant

is talking about our father has my back stiffening and sweat breaking against my skin. Grant hasn't seen nor spoken to our father in over five years. This can't be good.

"I'll be there."

I don't even have to think about it. I'm running into motion. I hail a cab, not wanting to wait for a car. I'll have my bags packed up from the villa and shipped home. I'm halfway to the airport when I realize I left Olivia.

Fuck.

I'm such a fucking prick. I'm not good at this stuff. I've never really dated before, and I've certainly never had to worry about running out on a girl. I dial her number, needing to apologize profusely and hoping she understands. It goes straight to voice mail. I cue it up once more and again, it goes to voice mail. Hanging up, I don't leave a message. Instead, I call the lobby bar and a female answers right away. I ask her to tell Olivia that I've had a family emergency and had to leave immediately and to have her call me right away. She agrees.

I've done all I can do right now. I just have to focus on getting home to my dad.

CHAPTER EIGHTEEN

Olivia

I SIT AT THE TABLE, WORRIED AND CONFUSED. HE HELPED usher the paparazzi out and then never returned. Are the details of my past too much? Surely, he wouldn't leave me here by myself. No. He wouldn't. Would he? I don't know what to think or how to feel at this particular moment, but embarrassment quickly takes center stage.

The room is empty save for me, but I'll be forced to walk alone through the lobby bar where everyone saw me come in with Spencer. Now I'll just look like one of his companions. Not special enough to come back for.

A familiar pang of disappointment falls over me. The desperate need to be numb is stifling. There's a good reason why addicts continuously fall off the wagon. It's not just temptation. It's life. Sometimes it's too much to handle.

I stand on wobbly legs, forcing myself to walk out of here. It would be worse to have someone come and escort me out. I hope he's paid the bill because if not, I'm in trouble. I don't have a dime to my name right now. I'm

135

standing here in the lobby bar with a dress that he picked out and paid for and I've been left, discarded like trash. I feel like a prostitute more than ever.

I make my way to the front door, hoping to go unseen when I hear a voice behind me. "Excuse me, Miss? Were you with Mr. Lancaster?"

I slouch down, waiting to be utterly embarrassed. "Yes."

"Mr. Lancaster had to leave." She sneers down at me. "He paid the bill and said he's sure you can find your way back to your room. You want to talk to the maître d' because he's arranged for transportation home for you to the States when you're ready."

I blanch at her words. Surely, she doesn't mean he's *gone* gone? I know we just started dating, but he wouldn't just leave the country without talking to me.

I move lifelessly toward the villa, wanting nothing more than to crawl into bed and not get out. But I stop at the maître d' first. "I was told that Spencer Lancaster has a message here for me."

"Mr. Lancaster has arranged for you to stay here for as long as you'd like, and whenever you are ready, he's asked me to arrange transportation with his family's pilot to take you back to New York."

I cringe.

"Is everything all right, Miss?"

No. "Yes," I say solemnly.

"Please let me know if I can be of any assistance to you."

I nod and walk back to the villa. The hurt is unbearable.

Why did he just leave me? Wasn't our time worth, at the very least, a conversation?

I can't deal with any of it, so I throw myself into bed and sleep.

———————◆———————

My phone chimes next to the bed and I almost ignore it, but curiosity gets the better of me.

Lindsey: Where are you? You fell off the face of the earth. I'm worried. Call me now.

I ignore it and five minutes later it chimes again.

Lindsey: I have resources to track you down, you know. And don't think I won't do it.

I groan. She'd love that, I'm sure. I pick up the phone, ready to give her a quick answer back when the phone starts ringing. I looked down to see it's her. I answer.

"What do you want?"

"My God, you sound like death. Are you okay?"

"No. I'm not," I say lifelessly.

"Where are you?"

"Barcelona."

"Still?"

"What do you mean still?"

"Oh, honey, you know I keep up with my tabloid gossip. I saw you both on the front page of the *Expositer*. Are you still with Lancaster?"

"No, he left me here."

The line stays silent for a minute. "What do you mean he left you there?"

"It's a long story, Linds. I don't feel like getting into it."

She huffs. "Do you need me to get you out of there?"

I don't want to ask for help, I really don't, but I want to call and arrange to use his family plane even less. "Would you? I hate to ask, but I'm desperate."

"Absolutely. I'll take care of everything for you. Text me the address and I'll send a car and book you a flight."

The line goes dead, and true to her word, less than twenty-four hours later I'm back in London and in Lindsey's suite.

When she sees me her jaw drops. "Oh my God, Liv?" She runs to me. "You look awful."

"Gee, thanks."

"Tell me everything," she commands.

I sit on the couch next to her and tell her all the sordid details. She holds me while I cry. This Lindsey is so different from the one I've partied with for years. She's caring, gentle. An hour later she's ushering me back to the bedroom, suggesting I lie back down. I stop her before she can push me through the bedroom threshold.

"I don't want to lie around anymore. I can't. I need to forget Spencer Lancaster ever happened," I say.

"Okayyy, and how?" she says, lips pursed.

"Let's go out and party."

She narrows her eyes at me. "Do you really think that's a great idea, Livs? It's not going to help you forget, and it might even make things worse."

"Nothing could be worse. I just need a night to forget all of it."

"I think it's a bad idea, but if you're sure, I can arrange it."

"I am."

Four hours later we're dressed in the most provocative clothes we could find and headed back to Club X. When we get to the front of the line Lindsey turns to me.

"Olivia, promise you won't get out of control."

I raise a brow. "What the hell, Linds? You're being such a party pooper."

"I'm serious. You've come so far and I'm so proud of you. You aren't like all of the others, and I don't want you to go backward."

"Stop. Let's just have fun. Don't worry about anything, please?"

Her smile is forced, and I can tell she doesn't like my answer, but she shrugs her shoulders and follows me into the club.

Tonight I'll forget all about Spencer Lancaster.

CHAPTER NINETEEN

Olivia

'M THROWING BACK DRINK AFTER DRINK, BUT NOTHING IS drowning out the pain. I'm desperate to be in the fog I was once accustomed to. The fact that I have gone this long without a quick bump is amazing.

Lindsey has watched me wearily all night. I'm getting annoyed, but she did me such a big favor that I don't want to snap at her. I glance at Murph, and I raise a brow, signaling I want whatever he has. He looks at me questioningly. He knows I don't use anymore, but I know him. He's lacking morals.

Strolling my way, he saddles up next to me. "What's up, Miller? Looking to partay?"

"Got anything fun?"

"I've got everything from A-to-Z. Pick your poison."

"C for old time's sake?"

"You got it." He grabs me by the hand and leads me into another room.

My inner voice is screaming at me to turn back. It's

scolding me about how I've been so good and come so far. *Don't let a man send you backward*, it pleads with me. Like every time before, I squash it down and shake it off. This is what I need. It's the only thing that will help. Murph is going to help me feel nothing.

He sets up a line, handing me a rolled up bill. "All set."

I quickly snort in the white powder, immediately feeling relief. In a matter of minutes, I'll be ready to paint the town red and dance until my feet bleed. My smile widens until Lindsey comes flying in, face red in anger.

"What are you doing, Olivia Miller? Have you lost your mind?"

"I've got her. Chill out, L," Murph says lazily. "What do you care anyway? This is your typical Saturday night."

"It might be mine, but it's not hers anymore." She turns to me. "You had me believing that people could change."

"You don't know what I've gone through," I snap.

"Are you kidding me? I think of all of us I'd know what you're going through more than anyone. You think I don't know what it's like to feel like you've been pushed aside and left alone? That's been my life, Olivia. At least you have a loving family. I don't even have that. My parents can't be bothered to even spend time with me on Christmas."

I don't say a word. The cocaine already filtering through my system is making me numb to it all.

"Don't do this," she pleads.

"It's too late." I turn my back and signal for Murph to set up another line. I have no plans on stopping this party.

The next morning my head is pounding and my body aches worse than it did yesterday. I slowly sit to find Lindsey in a chair, staring at me.

"My head hurts."

"Good," she says flatly. "I don't feel sorry for you."

"Wow. Is this how we're starting the day?"

"I'm really disappointed."

I groan. "Get in line. Apparently, I'm a huge letdown."

She stands and walks closer to the bed. "I'm not sure what happened between the two of you, but you need to call him. What if this is all just some huge misunderstanding?"

A pained laugh escapes my mouth. "What could I have possibly misunderstood? I was with him, paparazzi came, aired my dirty laundry, and then he left. End of story."

"It just doesn't make any sense. He runs in the same circles as me. He might be straight-laced now, but he definitely hasn't always been."

"He hasn't attempted to reach out to me. All I got was a message saying he'd pay for my room and get me a flight home." Like some cheap whore. In hindsight, I guess I am.

"It's been a little over twenty-four hours, Olivia. It would take about that much time to get back to the States."

"If that's even where he went," I add.

"I care about you, and you're making some bad decisions right now. Do you want to talk about last night?"

"What's there to talk about? You've already made it clear that you aren't impressed with my decisions."

Small lines start to crinkle in between her brows. "Do you plan to fall back into those old habits?"

"If I do?"

"Please don't. I like having one decent friend."

I roll my eyes. "I'm far from decent."

"You are the best person I know, Olivia. You have a chance to escape this life. Don't look back."

Her words hit me hard. I *have* come so far. I've managed to leave this lifestyle behind once before, and if I'm being honest, the temptation wasn't as bad. Why? Because I stayed away. As much as I don't want to admit it, I need to go home. My family has their shit together now, so what's stopping me?

"Thanks for everything, Linds."

Her cheeks turn pink. I don't think Lindsey is used to compliments or praise of any kind, and it makes me sad for her.

"Do you want to come back to New York with me? Meet my family? They'd love you."

She looks up, uncertainty clear in her eyes. "I don't know. I'd just be imposing. I could get a hotel room close by," she says hopefully.

"No, you'll stay with me. You can come to Sunday night dinner. My family will insist." They will. My family is great, and they would love to have her. Besides, with Bridget at school, there's an empty space at the table. Not that it would matter; they have a strict "the more the merrier policy." "Let's book our flights back sometime today. I need to get out of here."

She smiles. "On it."

For the first time in twenty-four hours, I feel lighter. Getting away from Barcelona and all the memories is what I need because forgetting Spencer is proving to be harder than I thought.

CHAPTER TWENTY

Spencer

I'M SITTING IN A PRIVATE WAITING ROOM . . .

Waiting.

I came straight to the hospital, exhausted and wanting information. All I know at this point is that my father was rushed to the hospital with symptoms of a heart attack.

My father is the strongest man I know. The thought of him being sick doesn't seem possible. He held our family together up until he retired. It was his decision to give me the company and withhold it from my brothers. He claimed it was in the best interest of the family. Grant didn't agree, and since then there has been an irreparable strain.

I lean back, running my fingers furiously through my hair. I'm frustrated at the lack of news. Where's my mother? To try to calm my nerves, I turn on the television. TMZ blares. I try to turn it off, but a picture has me snapping my eyes back to the screen. The girl that was with Olivia that night at Club X is plastered everywhere. Lindsey, the oil heiress. But it's not her that my eyes are fixed on. It's Olivia. At Club X. Seemingly having the time of her life.

Does she care about me that little? Surely, the hotel staff gave her my messages and filled her in on my dad, right?

I don't have time to contemplate it. The door swings open and my brother files in. My eyes meet my brother's for the first time in months. I suddenly feel awkward and out of place, but it doesn't matter because he comes right to me, enveloping me in a tight hug.

"He's going to be okay. Tell me he's going to be okay," I beg my brother to tell me. I'm usually the strong one, but not today. Not when it's my father who's in trouble. He's the glue to The Lancaster Empire. He might have retired, but everything I do is with his guidance. I don't know if I have it in me without him.

"Have you heard any news?" I plead once more for information.

"Mom sent me to get you. She's speaking to the doctor right now."

Looking around the waiting room, it dawns on me that Pierce is missing. "Where is he?" I grit out. Grant just shrugs his shoulders. My blood boils. *Where the fuck is he?* I want to scream. But Grant wouldn't know anyway. So I don't bother. "Tell Mom I'll be there in a minute. I have a phone call to make." He nods and walks away.

Pulling out my phone I dial my piece of shit brother. Straight to fucking voice mail.

"Get your pathetic ass over here," I hiss into the phone. My voice might be low because I'm in public, but there is no mistaking my rage. "You're a disgrace. Even Grant showed up. Even *fucking* Grant is here. You're an embarrassment to the Lancaster name." And with that, I disconnect. There's nothing more to say. After all I have done for him, all my father has done for him, he should have been here.

I pace for a minute. Inhaling oxygen to calm myself. Eventually my pulse returns to normal and I move to walk to the private room where they are keeping my father. Our mother is hunched forward in a chair as the doctor pats her back. She looks so sad and despondent. *What if she's not getting good news?*

She looks up at me, forcing a tight smile. "Spencer," she calls weakly.

"What's going on, Mom?"

She looks at the doctor, who proceeds to tell me that my father has suffered a heart attack and had to undergo a triple bypass surgery. "We were able to clear the blockage. Your father should recover."

I let out the breath I was holding.

"He'll have to take it easy for a long time and have routine check-ups, but he's going to be fine."

I sigh, relief washing over my body. I take my mother into my arms, holding her tight as she cries. My parents have a perfect marriage. A billion-dollar company to control can cause a rift like none other, but it never has with them. He was absent most of my years growing up and my mom has always stuck by his side and defended him. I always knew she loved him with all her heart, but in this moment, though, I can see just how much.

It makes me think of Olivia. The image of her in the club has me sobering. I know her. We might have only just met, but I know her. She wouldn't be out partying if she knew about my dad. There is no way. That woman would claw her way here to be with me.

So if she's there, what does she think is going on?

When I still don't hear from her the next day I'm even more pissed. Between her and Pierce I'm a live wire.

"What the fuck do you mean she checked out? I was supposed to get a phone call the minute she had a chance. What did you say to her?"

The villa manager is stumbling over his words. "I didn't relay the message, sir. One of my employees did."

"What?" I bellow. "I gave you strict instructions that the news should come from you."

"I'm so sorry, sir."

"I can't deal with you right now, but expect a call very soon."

I hang up on the man, ready to filet someone. Who

the hell talked to her and what did they say? I pull out my phone and dial. It goes straight to voice mail. I wait to leave a message, but her mailbox is full. This is playing out like some horrible drama.

I need to find her.

CHAPTER TWENTY-ONE

Olivia

DUE TO WEATHER, WE'RE FORCED TO LAND IN Trenton, New Jersey. Lindsey called in a car service for our long trip toward New York and my family's home.

"I just want to get there already," she whines.

"At least we aren't stuck in Trenton." I scrunch my nose at the thought. There's nothing wrong with Trenton. I just don't want to be stuck at any airport. Lindsey has a lot of money, and her family owns a private plane, but her father cut that off. Apparently, she was abusing the privilege. Doesn't surprise me. I can see how Lindsey could easily abuse her family's resources. I internally chuckle at the thought.

"What are we going to do when we get there?" she asks excitedly.

"Calm down, killer. There's not going to be much to do. I was kind of thinking junk food and movie night?" I shrug, waiting for her to freak out because I'm insisting that we stay in for the night. Instead, she surprises me by squealing.

"That sounds amazing." She beams. "I've needed a chill night for a long time."

"Netflix marathon?"

"That sounds perfect. I've been wanting to watch the rest of the seasons of *Gilmore Girls*."

"That can happen."

Lindsey knocks on the partition and it lowers. "Fargo, can you stop off at a grocery store somewhere? We need to stock up on some junk food." She winks at me.

I shake my head, laughing. She starts listing off all of her must get items, including ice cream, soda, Cheez-Its, and candy. I throw in a frozen pizza and her eyes widen.

"That's a thing?"

I raise a brow. "Um, yeah. Have you been living under a rock?"

"Yes, yes, I have," she jokes.

We're both extremely excited for our night of vegging out in front of the TV. I'm so relaxed at this particular moment, Spencer isn't even in my thoughts. I lean back into the seat, content on catching a few Zs while we make the trip to New York. I'm just about asleep when the car starts swerving erratically from side to side.

"What the heck?" Lindsey exclaims.

The next thing I know, my body's being hurled forward, and glass is shattering everywhere. I don't know what's happening, but my body is numb, and my eyes are closing. I hear sirens off in the distance and voices yelling. I can't make out what anyone is saying. It's all muffled. I strain to open my eyes, but everything is fuzzy and the pain . . .

Oh my God, the pain.

———•——

Sitting in the waiting room the next morning, my mom holds me in her arms as I remember being in the car, talking about Netflix and junk food, and then the swerving car and breaking glass. I was lucky. After only a few hours in the ER, I was cleared to leave. Only minor cuts and bruises. My body still aches from the jarring of the accident, but nothing Motrin won't take care of.

"Do you think she'll be okay? Why won't they let me see her?" Her lack of answers is starting to grate on my nerves.

"Do you want me to get you a snack?"

"Mom, stop trying to change the subject," I demand. "What do you know about Lindsey? Did Dad tell you anything?"

"I don't think it's a good idea for us to talk about it right now."

At that, the tears begin to fall. "Mom . . . please. Is she all right? Please just tell me she's all right."

My mom pats my head like a child, running her hands down my hair in a soothing motion. "They're doing all they can for her. She was hurt very badly."

I suck in a breath that manages to light my entire body on fire. Everything hurts, but I can't focus on that right now. "Is she going to die?"

"I honestly don't know, Olivia. She's in critical condition, and there's bleeding on her brain, but she's working with the best doctors. Her mom and dad have called in the very best for her."

"They're here?"

"Of course they're here. I think there in Lindsey's room with her now. "She looks puzzled by my reaction. "They're worried sick about both of you. Her mother's been in the chapel the entire time praying. She can't stop crying. I can't imagine what she is going through. It's awful about Lindsey, but everyone is so happy you weren't hurt. We love you so much."

"I love you too, Mom." I take her hand in mine and squeeze it.

"Do you want me to take you home? There won't be any answers about Lindsey for a while. You need to get rest."

"No, Mom, I won't leave here until I hear something. Then I won't leave either."

"Love you, Mom."

"Love you too."

CHAPTER TWENTY-TWO

Spencer

MY DAD IS BEING RELEASED TODAY AND TAKEN home to be put on bed rest by my mother. The poor man—figuratively, only fucking figuratively—will be lucky if he gets five minutes of alone time in the next month, but secretly I think he likes the way she's doting on him.

I'm getting ready to leave the hospital when Grant approaches me. He looks a little weary now that our father's in the clear. We've settled back into our awkward relationship, much to my displeasure. I never wanted this discomfort in the first place. I only did what was my duty given to me by our father. He would have done the same, although he claims otherwise.

He places his hands in his pockets and walks up to me. "Thanks for answering my call that day."

I scrunch my nose. "What did you think I'd do? I don't hate you, Grant. Our relationship might be strained, but that doesn't mean you're not family. When you call and need me, I'll always come."

He nods. "You know it's the same way for me too, right?"

"I do." Regardless of what's been going on between us, we've always been there for each other. Nothing will ever change that he's my blood.

"I wish Dad felt the same way," he says under his breath.

I quirk a brow at him. "Things with him not getting any better?"

"When he finally came to and saw I was in the room . . ."

"What? What did he do?" The anger in my voice is evident.

"He asked me to leave."

"Is that why you weren't here yesterday?"

He nods.

"It's time whatever bullshit happened between you guys is over, because I need you, man. I need your help with Pierce. I can't control him, and things are getting really bad with him. I'm busy with The Lancaster Hotels right now, and I need the support."

He winces at the mention of our sore spot. It's been the elephant in the room, and I just laid it out there like it was nothing. "Yeah, I've been seeing the tabloids recently. It's not looking good. We definitely don't need to be dealing with any more PR nightmares."

"I agree."

"Maybe we need to sit down and have a brother to

brother chat with him?" he suggests.

"I think that's a good idea. I don't know if he'll listen to us, but we can try."

"Hey, I'm sorry about your girlfriend."

I cock my head to the side and narrow my eyes. "What?"

"I saw that your girlfriend was in a serious accident, or did you guys already break up?" The nonchalance of his words has me standing up straight.

"What are you talking about?"

"That girl you've been seen with lately, the one they were all on a witch hunt to find? Olivia Miller. She and her friend Lindsey were in a horrible accident. Her friend had to be life-flighted from South Jersey to Jersey Shore University."

"No. You're wrong." I start pacing the room. "Where the hell did you hear this?"

"It's all over the news. Haven't you been watching?"

"The news? Why the fuck would I? I've been busy here!"

I feel dizzy. On the verge of throwing up.

Grant grabs me by the shoulder and holds me in place. "Olivia is fine. God, man, I thought you knew," he says, running his hands through his hair. "I would've never said it like that had I known."

"I need to get to her. Thanks for telling me, bro."

"Whoa, man, you can't drive like this. You're a wreck. Let me call you a car."

"I don't have time. I have to get there." Be there for her.

"All right, but please be careful." His voice is stern. "You can't help her if you're in a hospital bed yourself."

I throw my hand in the air as my goodbye, not looking back as I run to get to Olivia's side.

CHAPTER TWENTY-THREE

Olivia

WHEN I OPEN MY EYES, LYNN, MOM, AND DAD are hovering over me in the waiting room of the hospital where Lindsey is. When Lynn sees my eyes are open, she leans over and places a kiss on my forehead.

"You had us all sick with worry. Bridget has been calling nonstop demanding to know what's going on, but we had nothing to tell her. All they told me was you were in an accident. I'm happy you're fine. I can't imagine how annoying she'd be if you weren't."

I have to laugh at my half-sister. We've only known each other for a short time, but she fits right in. She always has. It's funny how fate brings people into our lives we didn't even know we needed. My family desperately needed Lynn, no matter how she came to be a part of it. My dad's indiscretions may have been hard for us to deal with, but Lynn is the one shiny spot in it all. Even my mom adores her.

"I'm fine," I groan.

My dad chuckles at my response. "Yes, you are, and thank God for that, Olivia. You barely have a scratch. Do you know how lucky you are? Be thankful it's not worse. Lindsey wasn't as lucky," he scolds, and I wince. The reminder that my friend is in critical condition makes me feel like shit for complaining.

"Is there any update on her?" I ask the room in general.

"She's been taken in for surgery. She'll live, but she's going to have months of therapy before she's able to walk."

I gasp. "It's that bad?"

"You have no idea how lucky you are."

I begin to cry at the thought of Lindsey being that hurt. She was there for me when I needed someone the most. She's become my best friend in a short amount of time, and her hurt is mine.

"Is there anything you can do to help, Dad?" My father is a well-known surgeon in New York and perhaps he can help. "Sorry, kiddo, not on this one. This is beyond my scope of practice. But I can assure you her parents are sparing no expense. Everything they can do will be done."

I relax, knowing they have all of the financial backing they need to get her the best care possible. I'm thankful that's the case. Many others haven't been so lucky. All of a sudden everyone in the hallway looks uncomfortable.

"What? What am I missing?" I demand.

My mom speaks up. "You have a visitor."

I scrunch my nose in confusion. "Who?"

"Spencer Lancaster."

I look in the direction of where my mom is looking, and there he is walking through the door into the waiting room. My jaw drops. "What? What's he doing here? How . . . How did he know?"

"Liv, it's all over the news. Everyone knows. You were with the heiress of oil," she remarks, raising her brow. "Clearly everyone's going to be covering it."

I groan. "Oh, God, this is horrible."

My dad speaks up. "Do you want me to send him away?"

"No!" I all but shout. "I just . . . I don't want him to be here because he feels obligated. I have you guys."

"Why would you say that?" Lynn asks.

I shoot her a nasty look, telling her to shut her mouth so no one else asks to know the details. I don't feel up to airing our dirty laundry.

"Relax, Olivia," Lynn says. "It's not like I'm not a sub-scription holder to *Exposé*. We know all about your tryst abroad with the sexy Lancaster."

My cheeks burn. "It wasn't a tryst. We were dating."

"Were?" my mom questions. "Clearly he thinks you still are."

My eyes widen. "Really?" I stop my words. My family doesn't need to know all the gory details.

"He's here, isn't he?" My mom looks to where Spencer is standing.

My dad grins. "Someone's been bitten by Cupid."

I cringe at his lameness.

"Seriously?" Lynn throws Dad a look of disappointment at his terrible joke.

"What? I have to say something embarrassing."

"Mission accomplished," I say.

"Coffee break time. Everyone out. I'm sending over the Sexiest Bachelor of 2017," Lynn jokes.

I roll my eyes at her now.

"What? Dad can't be the only one with the bad jokes." Everyone laughs at this.

It's good to be back with my family. I've spent so much time running away that I've missed out. I watch as they all quickly pile out, then I begin my internal freak-out.

He's here . . . He's actually here!

I have yet to look in a mirror since the accident. I've been so worried about Lindsey, I have thought of nothing but her. I'm probably a mess. I run my fingers through my hair, trying desperately to get some of the knots out to no avail. I'm still trying to tame the mess when he appears in front of me looking devastatingly handsome. His face is full of worry and my heart melts in this moment.

"You're here," I say softly.

"Of course I'm here." He comes to my side, takes my hand in his, and brings his forehead down upon them. "Are you okay?"

"I'm fine." I'm not. I'm still shaking, but having him here with me, I feel my pulse start to regulate. His arms engulf me, and his lips lay small kisses on the top of my head. He holds me for a minute and the beat of his heart calms me further. After a few seconds, he pulls back. His stare penetrates me.

"I heard about your friend Lindsey."

"She's hurt badly."

"I heard. I'm so sorry, Olivia."

"It's not your fault."

"Isn't it, though?"

I look at him, perplexed. "Why would it be your fault?"

"If I hadn't left you . . ."

"Why did you leave me?"

"I'm so sorry, Olivia. I should've called you. You have no idea how worried I've been."

"Why?" I deadpan.

He lifts his head to look me in the eye.

"You left me. Why would you be worried about me? Why are you here, Spencer?" I can't contain the bitterness from my voice.

"I didn't leave you, Olivia. I walked outside to get fresh air, and my brother called to tell me my dad had a heart attack."

My eyes widen at this news.

"I told the hostess to let you know and to help you get back to the room. I should've come back in and told you what was going on, but I just freaked. I didn't know how to handle the news." He shakes his head, looking tired. "I told you I wasn't good at relationships."

"Your dad had a heart attack? My God, Spencer. I had

no idea. The hostess made it sound as if you left me on purpose. I thought it was because of what the reporter said about my past."

He flinches. "Olivia, I'm a wealthy New Yorker. You think I haven't grown up with friends who have addictions? Look at Pierce. It doesn't define who you are now."

"So, now what?"

"Like I said, I want you. I want to be with you. I want to try this."

"You still want to date me? To be my boyfriend?" I sound so weak. So insecure. But why would he want this? Our time apart back in the real world reminded me who I was and who he is—and we don't fit. He's goddamn Spencer Lancaster, and all I am is a washed up model. My teeth nibble on my lip.

His finger tilts my jaw up. "Of course I do. Nothing's changed since I last saw you. I still want you. Why would I not?"

I think back to his face the night he left and what the paparazzi said. "I thought after what . . ." I trail off. "When I first started modeling, I had a coke problem."

"And now."

"No." And I don't. *Do I?* No.

"Have you done it since? Are you still using?" He isn't accusing.

"No." The words slip out of my mouth before I can stop them.

His eyes narrow, and with a shake of his head he leans

in and kisses me. I flush with heat. Even though it has only been a matter of days, I feel as if he's kissing me for the very first time. My stomach flutters at the soft press of his lips, the swipe of his tongue. As he pulls away, I can feel the smirk forming on his face.

"I needed to do that," he states. No apology for kissing me in a waiting room full of strangers. "So, what are the doctors saying about your friend?"

"She's supposed to be in surgery. We were just waiting for more information when you came. It's taking forever for an update. I just want to know if she's in surgery yet."

"I'll find out." He steps away and goes to the desk. Within a minute he's back in front of me. "She's being prepped right now."

My eyes begin to well. "Is she going to be okay?" I whisper, and he pulls me into him.

"She will," he states, not giving me any room for doubt.

We spend the next few hours in the waiting room, my head leaning on him. Eventually, I close my eyes and fall asleep. I'm not sure how much time has passed, but I hear Spencer through my haze.

"Hey," I mumble, my voice laced with sleep.

"I didn't want to wake you, but I wanted you to know she's out of surgery. She's going to be fine."

Fresh tears of relief pour out of me.

When we're allowed, Spencer escorts me to Lindsey's room. I peek in the door and go still when I see her lying there. She looks so fragile and small, nothing like the Lindsey I've grown to love. I grab her hand in mine. She's asleep and I don't want to wake her. I just need to see she's okay.

"Hey, Linds, that was hella scary, right?" I blow out a breath. "I'm so glad you'll be okay. They tell me you're going to have a long road ahead of you, but I'll be there every step of the way, I promise. You can count on me. You won't go through this alone." I sigh.

"Your parents are here. My mom says they've been really attentive and worried. Maybe when this is all over, you guys can sit down and have a talk? I really think you need to." I rub her hand comfortingly. "Demand they give you the type of attention you deserve. Make them see you want to be a family, because I know you want that, Lindsey. I see it every time you talk about them."

I squeeze her hand, and she squeezes back. I look at her hand and her fingers moving slightly. She doesn't speak, but I know she can hear me and that's enough for me. I place a kiss on her head and let her get back to resting. She's going to need a lot of it, but in the end, she'll be okay and that's all that matters.

When I step out of the room, I find Spencer waiting for me. He takes my hand in his. The warmth of his hand encases mine and makes me feel better. Like everything will be okay.

"How are you holding up?" he asks on the way out of the hospital.

"Fine. I'm just tired."

"You need rest."

"I needed to see Lindsey. I want her to know I'm here."

"You're a good friend."

"I care about her. She doesn't have a lot of people who do. Plus, it's my fault."

"It's not your fault."

"You don't know that." I caress his cheek. "I've been sick over the fact you left me. I knew I was falling for you, Spencer, but I had no clue how much."

He smiles. "Thank God. I thought I was the only one who had it bad." He chuckles. "I didn't think this was possible until the day I met you. I tried so hard to push you away because my life isn't easy. I've watched the strain on my dad. How stressed he was. How worried my mom has always been for him. I didn't think I ever wanted that. I thought I had to choose between a family or my career, and my career has always been a given." He takes a deep breath. "But now I know I want to try. Why can't I have both?" He throws his hands up. "For the first time I want both, and I want it with you."

I grin. "No need to rush, Mr. Lancaster. I'm not going anywhere."

He winces at my words. "Thank God. If something serious had happened to you, I don't know what I would've done. I would have never forgiven myself."

"Let's not focus on that. Let's move forward." He leans over and kisses me, and in this moment my world is right. Everything I want is in front of me, and I thank God I'm given this chance to enjoy my happiness.

Now that my world is perfect, I plan to help make Lindsey's the same. For now, though, I'm going to enjoy my man. "How fast can we get back to the city?"

He raises a brow. "What are you planning in that head of yours?"

"It's been too long since we've . . . you know."

"Had sex?"

My cheeks grow warm. "Well . . . yeah."

"I don't know if it's a good idea. You seem exhausted. I don't want to hurt you."

"I'm not porcelain. You can do it."

"I can definitely *do* it."

I roll my eyes. "Prove it."

Hand in hand, we enter the lobby of The Lancaster. This place is like nothing I have ever seen.

Standing tall, the building has large windows lining the front façade. The Lancaster faces Fifth Avenue and has a perfect unobscured view of Central Park. Prime real estate in Manhattan. I can't even begin to estimate how much this one property is worth, let alone the rest of the catalogue that comprises of *The Lancaster Empire.*

It's a bold statement, but as we walk through the pristine marble and glass lobby all the way to the private elevator that takes us to the penthouse suite, the message is clear. He's telling the world I'm his. That we are together. That he is taking me back to his place. It's funny to say that. We aren't going back to his place. We are going back to *his* hotel, The Lancaster.

As much wealth and opulence as I am expecting, I'm not prepared for what I'm greeted with. Not able to speak from pure awe, I take in the luxurious yet modern space. I know Spencer is rich, but this is a whole other realm of opulence.

"Is this where you live?" I ask as Spencer turns the key of a penthouse hotel suite.

"I don't actually keep a residence."

I turn my face away from the door and stare up at him.

"I don't understand. So where is it you stay?" I ask, the confusion evident in my voice.

"I'm never anywhere long enough." He shrugs as he pushes the door open.

"So you stay in your hotel?"

Spencer nods as he steps aside so that I can enter. The suite is magnificent. It doesn't even look like a hotel room at all. More like a luxurious apartment. Spencer takes my hand in his and he leads me down a small romantically lit hallway that opens up into a grand living room that boasts floor to ceiling windows on the far wall and on the other is a set of French doors leading into the bedroom.

"Come on, I'll make us something to drink." I take a seat on the couch and silence descends as he pours me a glass of scotch and hands it over to me.

"It is different, isn't it?"

"What is?" he asks as he lifts the glass to his mouth and takes a sip.

"Being here in New York. Together." For some reason I'm nervous. He gestures to the glass in my hand.

"Try it. It will loosen you up."

"Are you trying to seduce me?"

"Hey, you're the one who asked to come here."

"So, you don't want me?"

"Olivia, hear me now. It's taking every last bit of energy for me not to rip your clothes and fuck you already. To be so goddamn deep inside you that tomorrow you won't be able to sit without knowing I was there."

"So, why don't you?" I purr.

"Because I'm trying hard to show you I'm all in. That this is more than just sex for me. That I want you. All of you."

"Okay."

He steps toward me, his hand extends out until his finger sweeps lightly against my jaw. "Okay?"

"Yeah."

"So, let's have our first 'date' in the states. Do you want to eat?"

"I haven't eaten all day."

"Shit, why didn't you tell me? I would have insisted you

eat before you saw Lindsey."

"It's okay."

"It's not okay," he huffs out. "You need to eat."

"I can stand to lose—"

"Stop right there. You don't need to lose shit. And I don't give a damn what that fucking photographer said. You're perfect just the way you are."

I know I'm not, but I don't need Spencer lecturing me right now. I want to enjoy the time I have with him. "So, dinner? Since you own the hotel, do we get room service?"

"Since I own the hotel, you can get anything you want even if it's not in the hotel."

"Show off."

"You know it, baby."

Hearing him use the moniker makes me feel light, airy. It stretches throughout my whole body until I feel I can take flight.

After dinner, we sit on the couch, two glasses of wine on the table. His right hand reaches for my left and our fingers interlock. "Want to watch a movie?" he asks as his fingers gently skim my knuckles and causes me to shiver.

"Can we do that?"

"Of course we can. We can do anything you want."

I turn my head to him and cock it. "Really?"

"Again, did you miss the part where I own this hotel?"

He winks as a smirk spreads across his face. "And this is The Lancaster. We are known for our impeccable service."

"So, if I wanted to watch a movie . . ." I trail off, purposely letting him finish my sentence.

"We'd get it."

"And if I wanted popcorn?"

"Again, we'd get it. And Olivia, if you want those little candies all girls order on dates—"

"Jujubes."

"Yes, those. We'd get those too. Again, 'The Lancaster,'" he air quotes. "Anything you want."

"Anything?"

"And that, too. But not for all the guests. That's limited just for you."

"Good. I don't like to share," I say

"I don't share either." His voice is serious and I notice there's something in his eyes, something I can't place. It's lingering there like a dark cloud. Threatening to rain. "Come here." He pulls me close to him on the couch and I tilt my head up to welcome his kiss. A gentle one. When he pulls away, I pout.

"I promised you a real first date."

"We are in one of the nicest hotels in all of Manhattan, in what must be the most expensive suite. This isn't like a real first date."

"Just pretend we aren't. Pretend we just met and we just started dating."

"Well, that wouldn't be too hard."

"You're impossible," he says, and I laugh.

"Fine. I'm not a Jujubes girl, I want Reese's Pieces. Actually, no. I want hot popcorn with M&M's poured in the bowl so they get warm and crack a little."

"You're difficult, too."

"I believe the term is high maintenance."

"I believe you're correct. But lucky for you and me this is one of the simpler demands."

"I can't even imagine."

Spencer picks up the phone to dial his butler, runs off our list of supplies, then together we set out to choose a movie. Once settled, he pulls me into his lap and we eat popcorn and act like a couple of high school kids. It's the most fun and the most relaxed I've felt in the last few years.

Halfway through the movie, and with absolutely no notice, Spencer grabs my shirt at the bottom and pulls it over my head. He sucks in a breath as my breasts come into view.

"Sorry, this might not have been a good idea. I'm liable to ravage you. It's been too long."

"Please, ravage away. But while you're ravaging, take your time." I wink.

He removes my bra, tossing it aside. Taking my nipples in his fingers, he gently massages, drawing a moan from my lips.

"That feels so amazing."

He smirks at my words. "You haven't felt anything yet."

His soft lips take one into his mouth, sucking and massaging. Everything about his touch is gentle, yet rough. "You're so beautiful," he whispers against my skin. I feel his warm breath, his soft lips, and his hands roaming all over me. It's both pleasure and ecstasy. It fuels a fire until we're grasping and panting. Until we're both desperately trying to hold on to our wits and not overdo it, but the fuse has been lit and the fire begs to be unleashed.

And it is.

CHAPTER TWENTY-FOUR

Spencer

THE LAST WEEK HAS BEEN INCREDIBLE. BEING WITH Olivia has been incredible. I honestly never thought I'd feel this way, but it's so easy. If only all things in life were this effortless. Instead, I've been sitting in my office for hours, and not only do I want to bash my head against the desk, but I also want to fire everyone in sight. The Barcelona deal is still not closed. Not only is everyone dragging their goddamn feet, but another property I've been looking at seems to be outbid.

That makes two. Manchester, and now a property in St. Bart's that I've been eyeing. I had every intention of flying down to finish that deal, but this morning I got a phone call saying it was no longer available. This is a massive red flag that someone is purposely going after properties I'm looking at.

The door to my office opens and Jack walks in. Jack's official title is Head of Security for Lancaster Holdings, Inc., but I refer to him as the man who can find out anything.

And this morning at six o'clock Eastern Standard Time, I tasked him to find out who is going after my business.

"I got the information you were looking for," he says, and I look down at my watch.

"Took you five hours. You're slacking," I joke. This might be a new record.

"I don't think they were trying to hide who they were, boss."

"You're going to have to be more specific than that."

"The property in Manchester and the St Bart's property were both purchased by the same holding company."

"Okay."

"And it's obvious they wanted you to find out."

"Just spit it out."

"You're not going to like this, boss."

"Spit. It. Out," I hiss, knowing full well the name he's going to say.

"It was Grant. The same holding company that purchased the property to develop The L is the same company that outbid you on both of those properties."

"Fuck," I growl. I grab the snow globe from Vence that I purchased with Olivia off my desk and throw it against the wall. The sound ricochets and bounces in the silence of the room. Liquid streaks the wall and pools on the marble floor. This knowledge changes everything. Here I thought we were on the road to mending the bridge, but instead, he's burned the whole thing down.

Lucy runs into my office and looks at me, and then at

the wall. "I'll get that cleaned up right away."

"No, it can wait. Get my brother on the line."

"Which brother, sir?"

"Grant."

***

By the seventh time Grant's phone goes to voice mail, I'm seething. The bastard obviously knows I know it's him and has no intention of owning up to it. I'm at a loss of what to do. I need to expand. Expansion is the only option for the business to grow. We can't allow the business to be stagnant. If we don't grow, we'll plateau. We need this. I need this. I need to be able to bring Lancaster Holdings to the next level, to make it my own. To put my stamp on the future and be remembered for something. My father is my hero, but living under his shadow is daunting. The foreign market was to be my legacy, yet every step I take, my brother is there to rip away my progress.

Pulling at my roots, I ponder whether there's anyone else who's still loyal enough so I won't have to call *her*. Having to meet with her in Barcelona was hard enough. But to do another deal, that's just pouring salt in my wounds. *She* made me the man I am. Her lies and deceit made me this way. She's the reason I'm bad at relationships. The reason I have a hard time trusting.

I have no choice, though. She'd never choose Grant over me. *Addison Price*. The girl who ruined me for all other women . . .

Until now?

For the first time since Addison broke my heart, I'm actually enjoying being with someone, so maybe I'm not that broken after all.

CHAPTER TWENTY-FIVE

Olivia

FTER SPENDING THE DAY RUNNING MUCH-NEEDED errands, I'm ecstatic to see a message from Spencer asking me out to dinner. A mixture of anxiety and excitement courses through me. Tonight will be our first time out in *public* together since I've come back home to New York City. Sure, I've been to his place every night for the last two weeks—ever since we've been back from Europe—but Spencer and I have wanted to keep a low profile after the last time. Tonight will be the first time we go out with targets on our backs, putting ourselves in front of the paparazzi *again*.

Strangely enough, though, the press isn't the most nerve-wracking part. The nerve-wracking part is that tonight will be our first time testing our relationship in reality and not in the fantasy world we created for ourselves. Because that was what Europe was for Spencer and me.

A fantasy.

A dream.

And at times a nightmare I hope never to relive.

It hurts to think back to that night, so I try not to. But like a nagging thought, it keeps replaying in my head. The feeling of not being enough, of being left. The need to numb me.

I can't let myself go there. I can't let myself be that weak again. So I shake off the thoughts taking refuge in my mind, and instead, envision the night ahead and wonder to myself if tonight will fare any different from our previous outings? Will he be the same Spencer I have grown accustomed to in the privacy of our bubble, and more importantly, will I be the same Olivia?

An hour later, I arrive at the restaurant where Spencer texted me to meet him. I'm a few minutes early, and I pull out my phone when I see him walking up to me. Something is wrong. His brows are pinched and his body is stiff. He still swaggers as if he owns the world, but after getting to know him in Europe and spending the last few weeks in his bed, it's obvious something is amiss.

"Are you okay?" I ask.

"Just kiss me. I need you to kiss me."

I hope he'll tell me soon what's eating him up, but I respect him enough to not ask again and just kiss him. Wrapping my arms around his neck, I place my lips on his. Our mouths open, and I swear it's as if he inhales me as he kisses. My hands can feel the muscles in his neck loosening as his body relaxes against me. After a few seconds, Spencer pulls away and looks down at me, bringing his hands up to cup my face.

"Hi," I whisper as his fingers caress my jaw.

"Hey," he whispers back. He pulls me in tighter and buries his nose into my neck. I feel the warmth from his lips, the curve of a smile forming. "I missed you today." His lips tickle the tender skin where his nose is buried as he whispers to me.

"I missed you, too."

"Come on, let's eat."

Still holding on to me, he pulls me into the restaurant and then drops his hand to place it on the small of my back. The pressure of his fingers as he escorts me to the table sends a wave of tingles down my spine.

I sit down crossing my ankles and feel him gently place his hand on my knee. He already looks better than when we first got here. Calmer. A part of me hopes it's because of me. Unfortunately, now that he's more relaxed, being out with him is having the opposite effect on me. I feel as if everyone is staring. As if there's a secret reporter from *Exposé* at the table next to us. I know I'm being crazy, but hey, you never know. Spencer Lancaster is New York royalty. The press follows him everywhere. I can barely breathe from nerves when the waiter approaches the table and smiles brightly.

"What can I get you guys to drink to start with?" he asks Spencer, and it's obvious to me and everyone around that Spencer commands the room. He's a force to be reckoned with, one that if I'm not careful, will rock my whole world.

Too late.

He already has.

CHAPTER TWENTY-SIX

Spencer

THE PAST TWO WEEKS HAVE BEEN A LIVING HELL.

The news that my own brother is trying to sabotage me has really fucked with my head. What's worse than him going after us is that he did it after I thought we had made some progress. Serves me right for letting him in. Apparently, he hasn't changed, and apparently, my father is right about him. Every time I think about this or about Grant I get angry, and today I'm too tired to be pissed. I need a distraction.

Me: Come over.

Olivia: Bossy much?

Me: Not bossy enough. Bring clothes.

Olivia: Yes, sir.

I laugh. When Lucy calls me sir, it makes me feel old. When Olivia does, it makes me hard. The irony.

Three hours later, Olivia shows up at my place still dressed from whatever she had to do today. She looks hot as hell, but not at all dressed appropriately for what

I have planned.

"Get changed into something more casual. We're doing something a little different than hanging in my suite today."

Olivia raises a brow. "And what, pray tell, do you have planned?"

"Now that we're back in New York, I think we need to do typical New York things."

"And typical things would be?" She leans forward and I catch a peek of her full breasts. I groan at the sight, desperately wanting to rip the shirt from her body and have my way with her right here. She smiles, probably knowing full well what's going through my mind.

"We're going to a Yankees game, obviously."

"Seriously?" she squeals. "The Spencer Lancaster goes to baseball games?"

I gape at her. "I'm a warm-blooded male, Olivia. Clearly, I attend Yankees games." She smiles at my consternation. "Be ready in twenty. We'll have to leave soon." Without looking at Olivia or her amazing tits, I turn on my heel and walk out of the room to cool down.

Twenty minutes later, Olivia comes out wearing a short pair of frayed jean shorts and a tightly fitted New York Yankees tank top. Her hair is pulled into a ponytail high on her head.

Fucking hell.

"I see I have a Yankees fan on my hands." My voice comes out low and raspy, dripping with want.

"You're not the only New Yorker in this relationship."

I smirk at her sass. "You could've been a Mets fan." I scrunch my nose. "Then we would've had to rethink this entire relationship."

She scoffs. "I live in Manhattan. No chance."

The temptation to cancel our plans and stay in bed all day is growing stronger by the minute. This woman is the sexiest thing I've ever seen, and she doesn't even have to try. My balls are aching and sweat forms on my forehead.

Jesus Christ, Lancaster. Pull yourself together.

"Let's go before you strip me naked and we never leave," she teases, signaling I have no poker face when it comes to what she does to me.

Thirty minutes later we're seated in the outdoor suite that I've reserved for today. A few members of my executive team will be joining us, but for the most part, it's just Olivia and me enjoying some good ol' American baseball.

I see Olivia staring at me out of the corner of my eye. "What?"

"You look so . . . normal."

I laugh. "What does that even mean?"

"I didn't mean that in a bad way. You look . . . hot." Her cheeks redden.

"Hot?" I frown.

She leans into my ear. "I should've let you devour me back at the suite."

I squirm at her words, needing to readjust as my dick lengthens. "Olivia," I groan. "Not here."

She giggles. "You should wear hats more often." She flicks the bill to my Yankees hat. I wave her hand away, pulling the cap lower over my brow. At that moment, a man comes along offering food and drinks. Olivia looks at me in question.

"Two dogs, two Bud Lights, and a bag of peanuts," I order. Olivia stifles a laugh. I turn to her questioningly. "Is there a problem?"

"You're acting so normal."

"That's the second time today you've accused me of being normal. I'm not sure that's a compliment."

"I love it. We should do New York things more often." Her smile is wide and contagious.

"We will. I promise." I lean in and capture her lips.

At some point while we are distracted during the bottom of the sixth, the Yankees hit a homerun and the crowd grows wild. Olivia and I jump to our feet, cheering with everyone else. High-fives are offered to those around us and we all cheer for our team.

Olivia looks in her element. Watching her carefree and having fun is quickly becoming one of my favorite things. I'd do anything to see her like this always. *Man up, Lancaster. You're sounding like a love-sick asshole.*

At that precise moment, Olivia grabs my hand in hers. I've never been one for public displays of affection of any kind. The only time the paparazzi found me in that position was when I was at a club trying to score a piece of ass and they caught me at the wrong time. But with Olivia, it seems I'm kissing and touching her every chance I get. This is different. Olivia is different. I want to give her the world, and that scares the fucking shit out of me.

"Spencer," a smooth familiar voice croons from the seat above. I look up to see Addison. *Fuck.* When we met earlier in the week, she made it very clear she wasn't going to drop the idea of how "perfect" we'd be together. I barely got out of the meeting unscathed. At one point I even had to remove her hand from my own. I need to get out of here before this becomes awkward with Olivia. Turning my attention to Olivia, it's obvious it's too late for that. Her fingers tighten around mine, damn near cutting off the circulation.

"Hello. I didn't realize you were coming today." I try to sound nonchalant, but by the way Olivia is looking from Addison to me, she doesn't believe I didn't know. That or she's trying to figure out who Addison is to me. Nothing. That's what. Just a woman I'm unfortunately doing business with.

"I wouldn't miss a chance to see the Yankees play. Besides, today is a beautiful day." Her eyes blaze when they land on my hand in Olivia's. "I'm Addison." Her voice is sugary sweet, but I know better. She's a praying mantis. She lures you in with hopes of love but once she's had her fill she'll eat you alive.

Olivia's eyes narrow as she extends her hand. "I'm Olivia," she mumbles. But I step forward and take her hand back. Staking my claim.

"My girlfriend," I clarify.

"Lancaster." Gerald Walter nods at me.

Fucking idiot. He's a financial advisor for Lancaster Hotels. My father hired him last year and I've yet to get rid of him. He's good at what he does, but he's a complete douche. I had heard rumors that he ran in the same circle as Addison. Knowing her, she came with him to try to make me jealous. Or maybe they're dating and she hasn't changed at all. Clearly, there's more to the story.

I don't care to find out.

"We're actually getting ready to head out."

"We are?" Olivia asks, surprised.

"Yes, I have plans for us." I grin wickedly. "It was nice seeing you, Addison." I stand, pulling Olivia with me.

After a minute of walking, we're free from prying eyes, I pull Olivia into me and kiss her hard. All the pent up want from today comes through in this kiss. When I pull away, Olivia is blushing and breathless.

"What was that for?" she says, touching her swollen lips.

"I couldn't wait another second. I've wanted you all day." Olivia stiffens beneath me, her body going rigid. What the hell? What just happened? Pulling away from me, I look at her and see that her eyes have narrowed slightly.

"Who is she to you?" she whispers. *Where did that come from?*

"Who?"

She lets out an exasperated huff. "You know exactly who I'm talking about. What other girl did we see? That girl. Addison. The one *you* didn't introduce me to." She puts emphasis on the *you* and I feel like a complete asshole because she's right. I didn't and in return Addison did. "Why did she look familiar?"

God, I didn't want this to happen. I'm not prepared to share my history with Addison. Especially now that I'm doing so much business with her, I don't need Olivia getting paranoid and jealous. I'm already under enough stress.

"Come on let's talk about this in the car." Together we walk in the direction of where my driver is parked but we don't hold hands this time. Olivia is clearly pissed. As soon as the door is open and we are inside, she turns to me.

"So . . ."

"She's just someone I do business with," I say, trying to diffuse the situation without giving too much information. When she doesn't speak right away, I kiss down the swell of her neck again.

"Barcelona," she mumbles under her breath, more to herself than to me.

"Yes," I admit, still trailing my tongue down her skin.

"Can you stop?" she huffs out, pushing me off. I look her in the eye.

"What?"

"I can tell she's more."

"We dated."

"And . . ."

"And what? What do you want to know? We grew up together. We dated. She cheated. We broke up. Not much I can say about it," I hiss out. I hate talking about that time of my life. I hate when people lie, and talking about Addison brings me back to a bad time. We might be good now, but it took many years of me doing business only with her brothers before I was able to even be in the same room as her. Lying is a hard limit for me now.

"How long ago was that?" She speaks in a weak whisper, but no matter how low her words come out, there's no mistaking the hesitancy in her voice. She doesn't want to know and I don't want her to know either. I don't want her to know just how much Addison meant to me. How I loved her. How I thought I would marry her.

"A lifetime."

"Do you still—"

"No, Olivia. I don't have feelings for her. I'm with you."

"I just thought—"

"Don't think."

Her mouth drops open as she flinches at my words.

"Take me home," she spits out as she crosses her arms protectively in front of her body.

"Olivia." I incline my head and reach out to touch her. "I don't want to fight with you."

She sits quietly for a moment and then lets out a long puff of oxygen. "I don't want to fight with you either."

"So let's not."

"This is so new Spencer. I don't really know where I stand. You know the situation with my father. I don't ever want to be my mother, blindsided by another woman."

"I would never do that."

"I hope not but when you're obviously keeping a secret, how am I not supposed to be worried?"

"Like you said, we're a new relationship and I don't like talking about her. So I didn't."

"But, you lied when I asked you. That's not okay with me."

"Fuck." I pull at my hair. The thing I hate most is a liar and here I am lying. She's right. I'm not better than everything I hate. "You're right. I'm wrong. I don't give a fuck about her other than business. But please, Olivia let's not let her ruin a good day. Let's just be *normal*," I say. Hoping it reminds her how much fun we were having before our run in with my ex. The space between us grows silent again. A few minutes must pass before she finally speaks but when she does, I know I've won her back.

"I'd like that," she says and she shimmies over to me and places her hand on my lap. "I'm sorry for being so insecure."

"Don't be. It's me who should be sorry. And I can't wait for a chance to make it up to you.

"How about now? I can't wait to get you home." Olivia starts to run her hand farther up my thigh.

"Actually, we might not make it," I warn.

"Well . . . there's a screen divider in the back of the car." Her voice taunts me, making me want to do perverse things to her right now. I inhale deeply to stave off the massive erection she's inducing. This girl drives me crazy and I plan to blow her mind.

When we're finally back in the suite, Olivia stops in front of me, leans forward and places a soft kiss to my lips. "Thanks for taking me today," she mutters against my mouth.

"Even though I was so normal," I say as our lips separate.

"I love when you're normal." As the words leave her lips, her cheeks turn pink.

"Good. It's easy to be normal with you." *Did I just really say that out loud?* Being with Olivia is messing with my mind. I'm acting like a high school girl, wanting to talk about my feelings.

Her brow furrows at my comment. "What do you mean?"

"Just that it's easy."

"Elaborate please." *Shit, she's not going to let it go.*

"How do I explain this?" I move in front of her and look straight into her eyes. The way she looks at me is unnerving as if she's trying to search my soul. And the way my heart thuds in my chest, it's as if I want her to.

"You take me for what I am. I don't need to be anything else. Not the suit; not the boss. I'm just Spencer and I like it."

Her lips find mine. "Me, too. Now stop talking, Spencer Lancaster, and make love to me. Like a normal guy would."

"Now, that I can do." I want to say more but I don't. The truth is she's the first woman since Addison that's held my attention. That's made me want more. Addison did a real number on me. I never thought I'd want to date again. She was my best friend, but more than that, I thought she was the love of my life. Obviously, I was young then and I didn't know shit about shit. Boy, did I learn my lesson. Finding the girl you hope to marry fucking some other dude will do that to you. It wasn't until I met Olivia, that I even considered trusting another woman again.

Picking her up in my arms, I lift her and walk us to the bedroom before laying her down and crawling on top of her. I kiss a path down the side of her neck. And with that, I crawl down her body, but before she can protest and make me talk even more, my tongue juts out finding her hot and ready for me. I don't want her to talk, I just want to make her scream. And with the first swipe against her swollen skin, she loses all her words.

She loses all reason.

Which is good, because I'm already lost in her, too.

CHAPTER TWENTY-SEVEN

Olivia

T HINGS WITH SPENCER HAVE BEEN A LITTLE OFF SINCE the baseball game. Sure, we've seen each other, and we can't keep our hands to ourselves, but something isn't right. Before the game he was stressed, always having late meetings, and when I did see him, it took some time to unwind. I have known for some time that something is bothering him, I just don't know what. Maybe I just have too much time on my hands now that I'm not working. Maybe I'm just being crazy. But a part of me wonders if there is something more to the Addison story. Is he still in love with her? The idea makes me feel sick. I can't imagine losing him.

The need to learn everything about them is all consuming. So I do what any crazy, insecure, jealous girlfriend would; I Google. Bad idea. Really bad idea.

First and foremost, the woman is drop dead gorgeous. She makes most models, including myself, look like trolls. Secondly, she is an heiress to one of the largest property owners in the world. And if all of this information isn't making me want to bury myself alive in a ditch in Central Park, she also happens to be the best human being on the planet. She is the ambassador to UNICEF, and she spent a year building homes in fucking Zimbabwe, for crying out loud. I couldn't make this shit up if I tried. I click a few more links and the familiar need to numb myself creeps up, gnawing away at the carefully structured wall I have created since my slip up.

Exposed: A Happily Ever After In The Making?

Are two of Manhattan's royal families finally reuniting? That's the question on everyone's minds these days. The Princess of Property, Addison Price, and Hotel King, Spencer Lancaster, were spotted getting cozy at yesterday's Yankees' game. Sources close to Price say they have been spending a lot of time together both in and out of the office.

So the big question is . . .

What does this mean for Spencer's flavor of the month, Olivia Miller?

We can't wait to report.

My vision gets blurry as unshed tears collect.

Breathe.

Breathe, goddammit.

You were there. You know this is horseshit. Calm the fuck down. It means nothing. It better mean nothing. Reaching across the night table, I pick up the snow globe we got in Barcelona and I shake it.

Once.

Twice.

Three times.

The snow drifts inside the glass. The image of a perfect time is fuzzy and unclear. I wonder how long it will take to settle?

I flop back on my bed and close my eyes, trying desperately for the images of Addison Price and Spencer to fade away. But jealousy is a wicked thing. It creeps up inside of you like a vine, feeding on your insecurities. Playing off your fears. It's hard not to allow it to take over. To not allow it to strangle you.

An hour later and I'm still lying on my bed overanalyzing their relationship when the phone rings. It's my old agency. The first agency that ever signed me.

Why are they calling me?

My last few gigs weren't even through them as I was sure they would never call me again after "Incident runway." They wouldn't touch me with a ten-foot pole for the last few years, and with the fact I'm no longer rail thin, I can't possibly understand what they'd want.

Needing to know what they have to say, I swipe it up.

"Hello."

"Olivia."

"Yes."

"It's Lucinda." The sweetness dripping from her voice has my stomach turning, but I can't be rude, and I certainly can't not take this call. All my contacts have dried out and I need work. Not that my parents wouldn't support me if I needed, but the idea of crawling back to them, telling I couldn't hack it made me sick to my stomach.

"Hi, Lucinda. How can I help you?"

"I heard you were back in New York, and I happen to have the perfect opportunity for you. Would you be interested?"

I want to tell her no. To tell her to fuck off and I don't want her stupid campaign, but that isn't a wise idea when I have no other options. Plus, it's obvious all I'll be doing if I don't say yes is micro-managing every single thing about Spencer and Addison.

"What's the gig?"

"It's a lingerie shoot. New luxury line."

These are campaigns I hate, but unfortunately, am always asked to do because I'm tall and my breasts are still full. With the right photographer, I'm perfect, but I can't do this now. My body isn't what photographers want. I have curves, I'm healthy and in turn, I'm also undesirable.

"I don't think I'm the right person for the job, Lucinda, but thank you for thinking of me," I say, wrapping my hands around my middle. I'm not good enough for the job, I should say, but I'm way too mortified to admit that.

"It's not bras. It's robes and teddies. You'd be able to hide a lot. It's photoshopped."

Embarrassment and shame flood me. "Okay, I can do it," I say before I can stop myself. I'll just have to eat limited carbs. I shouldn't have to limit shit. I'm not fat and the fact that it's implied that I am, is horseshit. But what choice do I have. It's not right. I know it's not right. Agreeing to this shoot could very well be my demise but I need it. I need this job.

———⋅◦⋅———

A week has passed and I've managed to drop a few pounds before my fitting. Double workouts and limited carbs— okay, *no carbs*—have done the trick. I've spent the last four days following a strict diet program of asparagus and grilled chicken for breakfast, lunch and dinner.

Physically, I feel pretty good about myself when I walk into the studio. I've managed to do what Lucinda told me to. Mentally, though, I acknowledge that I've been pulled deeper down a rabbit hole I had no business dipping my toe into. We're shooting in the old loft space where the walls are a natural brick and exposed metal beams line the ceiling. A stark white bed with lush pillows decorating it sits in the middle of the space. It's pristine and perfect, and I want to tear it apart and hide under the sheets when I see a few of the models already in the room.

Patrick, the photographer, is fidgeting with the lights. I go behind the curtain and he begins shooting a girl I don't know. My gaze runs down to where her collarbone juts out, and suddenly I feel extremely out of place. But I have no choice, so I step out from behind the curtain, my full body on display.

I'm in a skintight teddy with a demi bra, and there is nothing left to the imagination. But as the makeup artist looks at me, I see how her eyes narrow. How she focuses on every imperfection marring my skin.

"Can you give her cheekbones?" one model whispers to the makeup artist. Tears prick the backs of my lids.

"Don't worry about them." A girl grabs my arm and pulls me back out of the way. "Patrick is a genius. He can make you look ten pounds skinnier." The comment should make me feel good, but instead, it serves as a reminder of how much I have let myself go, and just how much I'll have to do to get back.

With a shake of my head, I try to ignore her and put my best face forward. But hours later, we are working well into the night to get the perfect shot and I can't help but think it's my fault. Needing to freshen up, I walk into the bathroom and I come face to face with the same girl pouring a small bump of coke onto a key.

"It's going to be a long night," she huffs. Then she lifts the coke until it's directly below her nostril and inhales. *Got to keep it even.*

"Want some?" she asks. She repeats for the other nostril.

"I don't—"

"You should. We could be here for hours or longer. You won't get hungry," she says. An imaginary knife I have been feeling all day turns deeper inside me, forming lacerations.

I shouldn't

I can't.

But regardless . . .

I inhale.

After I'm done with the shoot, I check my phone. There's a message from Lynn. Bridget's in town, and they're going to a dive bar in the Meatpacking District. Lucky for me, I'm coming down from my high already and a drink will help take the edge off of wanting more. I respond I'll be there in thirty minutes and start to freshen up and make myself presentable.

When I get there, I see my sister standing by the door. Throwing my arms around Bridget, I engulf her in a giant hug. It feels good to be back with her. With college and my modeling career, it's been forever.

"Almost done," I state.

And her lips split into the largest smile I have ever seen. "Only two more finals and I'm officially a graduate."

"Are you prepared for your test, because asking Lynn and me to meet you at some dive bar doesn't sound like you're studying too hard."

"Girl, everyone needs a break. And dancing on a bar in cowboy boots channeling my inner Coyote Ugly is exactly how I want to decompress from the endless hours I have put into my degree."

"When do you go back?"

"Tomorrow."

"Shit. We better start drinking."

"Shouldn't we wait for Lynn?"

"Wait for Lynn for what?" a voice asks from behind. I turn to see Lynn with a smirk on face.

"To drink, of course," I chime in, and just like that it's as if no time has passed. It feels like just yesterday when I was with my kid sister and her best friend doing shots at a party. Who would have imagined how much our lives would change?

I wave my hand to the female bartender and order a round.

"To Bridget's test," Lynn shouts.

"To the Millers," Bridget exclaims.

Three shots down and I'm standing with my two sisters on the dirty, slimy bar. There's a trendy country song playing, and I'm pretending I know how to two-step. I'm about to fall over when my cell vibrates in my pocket.

Spencer: Where are you?

Me: Nowhere that you want to be.

"Who's that?" I hear Bridget scream across the music.

"It's probably her boyfriend," Lynn teases, her giggles sending me super-drunk vibes.

"Boyfriend? Dude, do you ever tell me anything?"

Lynn orders us another shot, which we quickly take before I recheck my phone.

Spencer: Try me.

Me: I'm with my sisters. Bridget is in town. She is

about to graduate, and we're celebrating.

Spencer: Where?

Me: You can't come here.

Spencer: Where, Olivia?

Spencer: Waiting . . .

Me: The Salty Pig

No way he's showing up here.

The song has changed once or twice, but my position on the bar has not. This time, instead of two-stepping, I'm jamming away to an upbeat pop song by some prepubescent boy.

"Who's the suit?" I hear Bridget say. Still shaking my hips, I open my eyes when two strong arms lift me from the bar.

"I'm her suit," Spencer says, putting me down and pulling me toward him until his lips touch mine. *Ohs* and *aws* sound throughout the bar.

"You're here."

"I told you, I miss you when I don't see you."

"I know, I didn't think you'd come here."

"Why? I wanted to see you, so I came."

"It's just not your scene."

"You're my scene. If you're here, then I want to be here."

I fall into the fierce gaze of his eyes and realize something . . .

Here in the dingy, dirty bar, I realize I'm falling in love with Spencer Lancaster.

CHAPTER TWENTY-EIGHT

Olivia

NOW THAT I'M OUT AND ABOUT WITH SPENCER IT'S as if everyone I used to work with and who snubbed me is coming out of the woodwork. First Lucinda, then Giorgio called to see if I could shoot with him in Milan, and now I've landed a high profile magazine cover.

Being in a relationship with New York's own king makes me a hot commodity, a shiny new toy for them to exploit. But beggars can't be choosy, so here I am at another job.

High as a kite.

What started as one bump to get through a night of shooting quickly escalated to two, and now it's mandatory if I'm on the job. I've also lost fifteen of the twenty pounds I put on when my career took a hit after the runway debacle. I wish I could say I'm strong enough to stop. That knowing Spencer might find out is enough to make me want to clean up my act. *It hasn't.* If anything it's had the opposite effect. Instead, I find myself using more and more.

I can't get through a shoot without a bump now. The pressure to be someone that would make him proud, to be successful is blinding.

Inhale.

I both love and hate this feeling. My heart pounds, adrenaline courses through me, and I'm restless. At the same time, I feel invincible as though nothing can stop me. As if I can conquer the world. When I walk into the shoot a few minutes after taking a bump, I might not be the skinniest model on set, and I might not be the prettiest, but I don't care.

I got this.

An hour later, all the pictures are taken and I'm starting to come down from my high. My anxiety is peaked. The itch to take another bump crawls on my skin.

Slithering around.

Begging me to take another.

To fall into the abyss yet again.

I need to get out of here. To get a drink.

I'm edgy.

Looking at my phone, I see Spencer texted.

Spencer: What are your plans?

Me: Finishing up.

Spencer: Come here. I want you.

Fuck. I can't go there now. Sure, I've gotten really good at hiding when I'm on coke, today is too much though.

Today, I'm too hopped up.

Me: Give me a few. Going to grab drinks with one of the other models.

Spencer: I'll let my staff know you're coming. Actually, I'll tell them to always allow you up.

Always allow me up. The words he's typed should make me feel warm and fuzzy inside. Instead, I feel awful.

I'm lying.

He would leave me if he knew.

If he knew what an awful person I am.

If he knew that I'm a fraud.

CHAPTER TWENTY-NINE

Spencer

"GOD FUCKING SHIT," I SCREAM IN MY OFFICE. Lucy is standing at the foot of my desk as pale as a ghost. It's not her fault. It's not anyone's fault. But here I am losing my shit once again.

I dial Addison's number.

"You can leave Lucy." She skitters out like a scared mouse. I want to call out to her and apologize but the phone is already ringing. It rings and rings. On the third ring, I hear her voice.

"Spencer," she drawls into the phone. "To what do I owe this honor?"

"Cut the shit, Addison. I know you talked to him."

"Talked to who? You're going to have to be a little clearer?" She's toying with me and I don't like it. Not one bit.

"You know who hell I'm talking about. Don't play games with me or you'll regret it."

"Tisk. Tisk. I don't think Daddy would like to hear

you're talking to me this way. Especially since we have so many deals on the line."

"What do you want, Addison. Name your price?" I hiss. There is no way I'm losing another property to Grant.

"Dinner."

"No."

"Drinks." She won't let this go. I know she won't. "We still have to sign the St. Barth's papers."

My blood boils. I want to bash the phone on my desk, but instead I take a deep inhale of oxygen, hoping that will be enough to calm me down.

"When?" I finally breathe out.

"I'm traveling. I'll be back in a few weeks."

"Fine." I hang up. Not even waiting for her to respond. She'll call me when she's back in town. If there is one thing Addison is, it's persistent.

Olivia is at the hotel when I get home from work. She's waiting in the lobby smiling broadly at me. I don't smile back. Just take her hand and lead her to the elevator.

"Hey, will you slow down?" I pull her faster down the hall until we are standing in front of my door and I'm opening it. "God. What the hell is wrong with you?" She's annoyed and rightfully so. I just manhandled her in the lobby, elevator and now in the hall. But I don't want to see anyone. I don't want to talk to anyone. I just want peace and quiet in my apartment.

"I don't want to talk about it," I growl. I don't. Today was shit. Grant is all over me. And I have no idea why.

What his end game is. And it's pissing me the fuck off. I like to be two steps ahead at all times. But with this, I feel like he's feeding me information when he goddamn feels like it and it's always two steps too late.

"Spencer, if something is bothering you—"

"God fucking dammit Olivia, I said I don't want to talk about it and I meant it," I snap. And even as the words leave my mouth they feel like bile, but it doesn't stop them from spewing out. She lifts her hands to touch me and I push her away.

"I can't do this now." She opens her mouth to object but I don't stay to listen. Just turn on my heel and slam the door behind me to go to the bar and grab a drink. I'm not used to letting people in. With most of my life being public knowledge, I'm used to keeping my feelings close to me. There are only a few people that have ever breached the wall I have erected around myself, Olivia is one of them. But sometimes, I fall back into old habits and just want to shut the door. Not have to answer anyone. It's been a long time I since I have let anyone one in, wholeheartedly. *Grant was the only one.*

Why is he doing this to me?

———————•◦•———————

An hour later, I find myself back in the suite. I'm drunk now. Piss ass drunk. When I argued with her, I left her. I went downstairs and drowned myself in scotch. Now

I'm back, and I'm barely in the door before I see Olivia. I don't speak, just saunter up behind her as she is bending over the counter grabbing a glass. I'm not sure what goes through me. This feeling I don't get. It's primitive. I need to be inside her. Mark her. As mine.

We fought.

I was nasty. Brutal really. But I don't give a shit. I need her. I need contact; I need to connect to her right now.

This is what I know.

Sex is what I know.

I used to know more. Once upon a time, I was in love and then it was killed. I care for Olivia. But love . . . no. I don't love her.

I need her.

I need her like I need air to breathe.

She's all encompassing and I need to consume her.

She must feel my presence because her body stiffens. But I don't allow that to halt my intentions. Instead, I reach my hands out, I trail them down her spine, over her hip, lifting her skirt.

"Fuck. Do you ever wear anything under your clothes?" Bare again. Always fucking ready for me.

"No," she moans.

My hand is cupping her, and my finger presses deep inside. She tightens around me like a vise. A vise that is begging to get fucked. I pull my hand away. She's primed for the taking. I pull my dick out. Gripping. Stroking.

I begin to press into her. It feels too damn good.

"Fuck," I mutter. "No condom."

"Clean, pill," she groans.

Hell, yeah.

Those two words are all I need. I slam in.

Giving her all my anger.

All my hatred.

Misplaced, but I give it to her anyway, and she takes. She takes it all. All I have to give.

Purring. Moaning.

Grinding up against me. Fucking me back.

It's hot.

It's primal.

I pound into her at a pace that will bruise. That must tear her apart, but I don't give a shit. I need this. She needs this, and I'm going to give it to us.

Thrust.

Thrust.

"Fuck," I shout. My body is seizing.

My world is going blank, as I empty myself in her.

My eyes begin to blur. The world spins. I pull out and barely register Olivia taking my hand, and she's leading me to the bed.

All goes black.

———————•———————

Shit, I was an asshole yesterday. I didn't mean to snap at her but between the shit with Grant and the bigger fucking shit with Addison, I'm a mess. Doing business with her is starting to become a liability not only to my business but to my health. Then I go and meet Olivia. She just came home from a job. Probably stressed and what do I do? I rip the fuck into her.

The fact that she forgave me, the fact that she's in my bed at all right now is a modern miracle. I attacked her like I was an animal.

It was primal and fuck if it wasn't hot as fuck.

The way her hair fanned the countertop as I fucked her from behind.

I don't deserve this girl.

I need to get my shit together. Get Grant on the phone, settle this. But instead it's eating me up inside, and I'm a dick.

I'm a dick in real life. But not to her. Never to Olivia.

I can see the distance start. She's been pulling back.

Maybe that set me off.

Maybe I am just an asshole.

I don't know. Guess it doesn't matter, damage is done now it's just what I'll do to fix it.

Me: Good morning beautiful.

I send the text. Imagining her lying in my bed naked. Great. How am I supposed to work right now imagining her naked in my bed?

Olivia: Morning.

She responds. I can't tell if she's still mad.

Me: Will I see you later?

Wow, I'm a pussy.

Olivia: I have work.

Me: Fine. Call me when you're free.

I slam the phone back on the desk. I need to get my shit together.

CHAPTER THIRTY

Olivia

'M LYING IN MY BED. A WEEK HAS PASSED SINCE I LAST saw Spencer. I don't know if I'm intentionally avoiding him or just working really hard. A part of me knows the answer. I can't see him now. First thing, he's not the same. He's angry. Quiet. I'm not sure if it's me. I can't tell and I'm too scared to find out. So I avoid him.

Other than the shit with Spencer, everything else in my life is actually coming together. Jobs are lining up. I'm finally catching a break on the modeling front.

My phone rings and I swipe at the screen. A name from my not-so-distant past flashes on the screen of my phone and I desperately want to send him to voice mail. *Bennett.* I should have guessed he'd be the next one to try to cash in my new notoriety. What does he want? *Probably to work with me again.* I haven't seen his name or even thought about him for years. Not since the shit show a few years back.

"Hello," I answer.

"Liv?"

"Yes."

"It's Bennett."

"What can I do for you, Bennett?" I bite out.

"No need to be testy. I just want to talk to you."

No need to be testy? I let out a huff of breath. The last time I spoke to Bennett, I ended face down on the runway. How I convinced my parents it was no big deal is beyond me, but somehow I managed to almost escape unscathed. I simply explained I had a few too many celebratory shots and somehow everyone believed that.

But I know the truth . . .

Booze and coke. Not a good combo.

"What do you want?" I ask again. This time my clipped voice makes him laugh.

"I want you to work with me again."

"Now why would I do that?"

"You owe me."

"I owe you what? I'm lucky I even have a career at all."

"I made you."

"So then go make someone else."

"I don't want anyone else. You're everywhere. I can't open a magazine without you and Lancaster on the cover. It's free advertising. I need you for this project I'm doing."

"I have to be honest, Bennett. I don't care what you need. I wouldn't work for you ever again. Not if you were the last photographer on the planet."

"You sure about that, sweetheart? You really want to

play this game?"

"I'm not playing games. I don't want anything to do with you."

"You didn't say that when you were coked up out of your mind and sucking my dick."

"I got to go."

"I wouldn't piss me off if I were you."

"What are you going to do?"

"Just try me."

"Goodbye, Bennett. Don't call me again."

"Don't say I didn't warn you." I don't like the threat in his voice and hang up quickly.

The biggest mistake in my life was getting involved with Bennett. But I was young, didn't know better. At the time, I needed something that was solely mine. Something I could feel proud of. Modeling was that outlet for me, and Bennett gave me that escape.

Unfortunately, like all things in life, it quickly morphed into something else—a toxic relationship that fed on my insecurities. Before long, I wasn't skinny enough. I couldn't work hard enough. But Bennett had something to help, and one night during a late shoot, he offered me the solution to all my problems.

I still remember the feeling after the first line. The burning down my throat. I choked as it singed my nostrils and then dripped like battery acid. But soon a feeling weaved its way through me. An unmatched euphoric feeling.

I was no longer Olivia Miller.

Being skinny enough or pretty enough didn't matter. What was going on back home with my family didn't matter. Nothing mattered. I was happy. I could conquer the world and I did. For some time, I really did. My bones stuck out, and I landed jobs left and right. Life was great, and with Bennett by my side, it seemed everything was perfect. But then one night everything went to shit. Bad coke . . . too much champagne . . . and I passed out on the runway.

The offers stopped after that. Runway shows were out. Trips to Milan—out. And Bennett . . .

Out as well.

He decided I was a liability to his career, so he dropped me as fast as everyone else did. Even hearing Bennett's voice brings me back to a bad time. Muscle memory maybe. The familiar ache gliding through my veins, wanting to silence the world. I shake it off. I pick up my phone and dial Spencer instead.

"Hey, beautiful." I hear through the phone. The baritone of his voice makes my insides melt with need and desire.

"What are you doing tonight?" I ask, sounding pathetic and needy but I need a distraction. Spencer is the perfect one. I don't think about my failures so much when he's around.

"Meeting, rain check?"

"Okay." I can't help the disappointment in my voice.

"If I could blow off this meeting, I would, but it's to discuss the St. Barth's property."

"I understand." And I did. It isn't his fault I'm rattled from my earlier conversation with Bennett. He has to work and I just have to deal with that. "Call me after?"

"Promise."

"Okay, bye." I hang up before he says the words. The screaming in my mind to detach is starting to hammer in my mind louder and louder. Before I can change my mind, I pull out my phone and text Murph.

Me: You back in town?

Murph: Yep. You looking to party?

Me: Yep.

CHAPTER THIRTY-ONE

Spencer

TODAY HAS BEEN FUCKING STRESSFUL.

The Manchester deal might have fallen through, but now that everyone and their mother has realized I am expanding into Europe, my phone hasn't stopped ringing. Every hungry real estate agent is trying to sell me land. They all know how much money the Lancasters have, and every person I have ever met is crawling out of the woodwork to sell it to me. Normally, I wouldn't meet with anyone I haven't done business with, but with Grant sniffing around Addison, I can't afford to not. So I have sat through meetings, presentations, and pitches demonstrating why I should buy, but after the last property disaster, I'm more cautious, careful.

As I sit back in my chair pursuing a property in Croatia, my stomach growls. *Shit, have I eaten today?* No, I haven't. I grab my phone off the desk.

Me: Have dinner with me.

Olivia: Can't.

Me: What are you doing?

Olivia: Errands.

Me: So, stop and meet me.

Olivia: No can do. Sorry, but I can come over after.

I look at the phone, my eyes narrowing. This is the third time in the last two weeks she's blown me off for dinner.

Me: You have to eat, Olivia.

Olivia: I will, Spencer.

I don't need to be near Olivia to know she's pissed that I'm on her case. I drop it.

Me: I'll be home. Come when you're done.

Olivia: Okay.

Something is off with her. I just can't pinpoint what it is.

Walking out of my corporate office, I head to the front of the building where my driver is waiting. Most would think my office would be in the hotel, but as we have a downtown hotel and so many other properties, most of our day-to-day business dealings for all the properties are handled at our Park Avenue building.

It's after seven o'clock when I finally make it to the hotel and up the private elevator. When I step inside, I see Olivia is already there, curled up on the couch. My butler must have let her in. A throw blanket covers her as she drinks a glass of the rosé I started stocking the moment I realized she liked it.

"I like seeing you on my couch when I come home

from work." As the words slip out of my mouth, I realize how true they are. I do like having her here, lying curled up on the couch, a minute away from falling asleep. *God, I have it bad.*

Her eyes dart open with surprise, and then her lips turn up into a smile. "I like being here when you get home."

Silence hangs in the air with this admission.

I take a step closer. When I'm standing in front of the couch, I look down at her and then take a seat.

"I missed you," she whispers as she climbs in my lap.

"I missed you, too." Leaning forward, I brush my lips against hers. "It's been too long," I say against her mouth. "How was work?"

I feel her stiffen. "Just working hard. Nothing to tell. Trying to make the big bucks. Got to have some money to spoil my boyfriend."

"You don't have to buy me anything or pay for anything, Olivia."

"Maybe I want to."

"Why are you working so hard?" When she doesn't answer, I pull back and notice she's nibbling on her lower lip.

"I just . . . Well, I guess since my parents didn't want me to do this, and then after losing the last job, I suppose I want to succeed."

"You don't have to prove anything." The hypocrisy of my words tastes bitter on my tongue. I work harder than anyone I know and for what? To prove something. But it doesn't matter. This is Olivia, not me. I don't like seeing her like this.

"I know."

"Do you?"

"Can we talk about something else? We haven't seen each other in days. Or maybe we don't have to talk at all."

"What did you have in mind?"

"Let me show you." She lifts her body off me, but only enough to arrange her hands on my waist and lower the zipper to my slacks. Leaning back, I close my eyes and wait for the pleasure of Olivia's mouth. Once engulfed, I can't think of anything but the pleasure she brings.

When I feel myself getting closer to release. I place my hand on her shoulder. "Stop," I pant, barely holding on. "Need to be inside you." She lifts off me. "Clothes. Off. Now." If I'm not inside her this minute, I might die. She makes quick work of her clothes. My breath leaves my body, but not in a good way.

"What the fuck?" I run my gaze up the length of her body, from her collarbone jutting out to the bones protruding from her hips. How have I not noticed this? How have I not seen how skinny she's become? Anger flares inside me, but not at her. At me. I was so busy working, I never saw what was happening. But now it all makes sense. She hasn't eaten with me in weeks. Not since she started modeling again.

"Are you eating?"

"Of course I'm eating."

"Then how do you explain your hipbones sticking

out?"

"I'm eating," she hisses as she works to throw on her clothes.

"What are you doing?"

"Leaving."

"So, that's it? I ask you a question you don't like and you leave?"

"Don't like it, do you?"

"What the fuck are you talking about?"

"You've been in a mood ever since we've been back home. You never talk to me. Never tell me anything."

"That's different."

Now dressed, Olivia places her hands on her hips. "How is it different?" she asks before pursing her lips.

"That's business. And this . . ." I place a hand on her collar. "This is your health, Olivia. I care about you. I don't want you to hurt yourself."

"I'm not. I'm just eating healthy and working out."

"That's it?"

She furrows her brow and then takes a deep breath. "Yes, that's it," she whispers, biting her lip. She looks as if she's about to cry. The sight breaks me.

"Come here." Olivia steps into my arms. "I care about you. If you ever need—"

"I'm fine."

Despite my better judgment, I let it rest. The last thing I want is to rock the boat again.

CHAPTER THIRTY-TWO

Olivia

TOSSED AND TURNED ALL NIGHT IN SPENCER'S BED, ALL of my lies eating away at my subconscious. When he asked me last night if I was eating, it was as if a part of me shut off. I didn't know what to do. I couldn't tell him the truth. I couldn't tell him what I've been doing to lose the weight. He'd never understand.

Standing, I pad my way through the bedroom and into the bathroom to freshen up. I'm dressed and brushing my teeth when I hear the sound of footsteps behind me. When I turn and face Spencer, everything inside me freezes. The way he stares at me is glacial. His green eyes hard as stone.

"What. The. Hell. Is. This?" he says slowly, the words coming out staccato. I have no idea what he's talking about but then he flings a copy of *Exposé* in my face and it all becomes clear. On the front cover is me, bent over a table half-naked and snorting a line of coke. But it's not a recent picture.

Oh my God.

Bennett.

He did this.

He leaked a picture to the magazine because I wouldn't work with him. My heart hammers in my chest. Every part of my body begins to shake.

"I can explain."

"You can explain." It's not a question. It's not even a statement. His voice is flat, uncaring. Brittle and cold.

"It's not what it looks li-like," I stutter. My chin rattles in my jaw.

"Oh, no? So, it's not my fucking girlfriend barely dressed at a photo shoot doing coke?"

"Well, it is that, but it's not what you think. It was before."

"So, you're not doing coke?" he asks and I don't answer. "It's not a hard question. It's either yes or no." My gaze settles down to the floor. "So, you are? Goddammit, Olivia. Tell me the goddamn truth. For once, tell me."

"It was only a few times."

"I want you out of here, now." His words are so loud, they boom off the walls around me.

"No, please let me explain—"

"Explain? Why should I? When I asked you at the hospital if you were still using, you said you weren't. Was that a lie too?"

"It was only—"

"It's a yes or no question, Olivia."

"Yes."

"This is shit I won't stand for. I made a promise to myself when my girlfriend cheated I'd never fucking deal with lies again. I have no choice but to put up with that shit from Pierce, he's my brother. But you? Who are you to me? No one, that's who," he spits out, and then goes silent. If possible, his silence cuts me deeper than any words could. Because his silence only means one thing . . .

He's done with me.

CHAPTER THIRTY-THREE

Spencer

IT'S BEEN A WEEK. I HAVEN'T ANSWERED HER CALLS, AND I certainly haven't called her. Instead, I've worked my ass to the bone, and when I'm not working, drank myself to oblivion. Like right now, that's what I'm about to do.

I lift the bottle to my mouth. No need for pretense. I'm not drinking to enjoy myself. I'm drunk because I'm pissed. She fucking lied to me. And if there is one thing I refuse to put up with, it's a fucking liar.

This is the reason I don't date anymore. It's one thing or the other. They're either out for my money or the acclaim that comes with being with me. That's the one thing I miss about Addison. It was so easy. I never had to deal with this bullshit.

Fuck.

I take another deep swig of the amber liquid. It burns my throat as it pours its way down. *This is pathetic. What am I doing?* I'm in my goddamn prime. Lord of my own empire and I'm sitting on my floor of the hotel drinking alone.

There are a million women I could call right now. Who'd be here down on all fours pleading with me to fuck them right now. But I don't want any of them. All I want is a blond haired, blue-eyed goddess who makes me insane at times.

I should call her.

But I don't.

I still need some time to process the lie. It's not necessarily that she did the coke, but the lie I can't get over. I've never been addicted to anything . . .

Maybe I was too hard on her.

Taking another swig, I pull my phone out and dial her number. Voice mail. She's probably getting high. The thought infuriates me even more. I reach for the bottle, but this time it's empty. Rather than call for another, I decide to head to the roof bar and grab a drink.

Once in the lobby, my phone rings. Addison.

"Lancaster here."

"Spence, do you have to answer that way. You know it's me. I certainly know it's you."

"Point taken. So, what can I do for you at . . ." I look down at my Rolex. "At nine p.m. on a Friday evening."

"I'm back in town."

"Your point."

"I need you to sign some papers."

"You do realize it's nine o'clock, right?"

"Oh, shut it, Lancaster." Her mocking tone over the syllables to my name has me laughing. "You're one to talk. You're always working. You work so hard you don't even have your own place. You just jump from hotel to hotel."

"I like it that way."

"You like the control. Don't want to pass over any reins to anyone else."

"I'm smart."

"You're a control freak. Don't you want roots?"

"Never said I wasn't. And no, I don't." Taking a deep breath, I calm myself. "So, papers. Can it wait until morning? I'm just going to Oak to have a drink."

"You promised me a drink. And a drink I will get. I'll meet you there."

When I step into Oak, the wine bar on the top floor of the building, the hostess greets me. "Hello, Mr. Lancaster," she purrs. "Your regular table?"

I nod. My usual table is a small intimate table in a secluded alcove overlooking the city. Small candles, sheer drapes and a stunning view makes this stand one of the most sought after tables in all of the city. But I'm the owner, so it's mine.

"Addison Price will be joining me."

She can't help but pout at the news. Word must be spreading through the hotel that Olivia and I are on the outs. It's the nature of the business. As tight a ship as I run so my guest's information won't leak, the staff loves to gossip about me. I bet she's hoping I'd close the curtain and show a bit of my wicked playboy ways.

My usual scotch is set in front of me by the time I make

it to the table and sit. Someone deserves a raise, that's for sure. I'll make sure to have my assistant give Jimmy one on Monday morning.

I'm halfway through my scotch when Addison arrives at the table. She slips in beside me, her body close to mine. The warmth of the liquid permeating my body has me loose and not wanting to do business, and as the heat of her body radiates off her, my body has a mind of its own.

"Addison." My voice is lighter than normal, and not as rough around the edges. *Must be the booze.*

"Rough night?"

"That's an understatement."

"Want to talk about it?"

"Not particularly," I deadpan.

She reaches her hand out and squeezes mine once before setting hers back on the table. "Spence. How long have we known each other? You can talk to me."

"Do you read *Exposé*?"

"Yeah," she pauses, her eyes peering into mine, "maybe it's for the best." She stares at me for a second, her body inching over to mine.

"What are you doing, Addi?"

She smiles at the familiar nickname I haven't used in years, and places her hand on my lap, dangerously close to my cock. So close she actually flicks it lightly with her fingertips. It stiffens against her in response, and she licks her lips seductively.

"I miss you, Spence. I miss us." Her hand covers me,

palming me. I'm painfully hard now, and drunk enough that I'm not sure I care that it's her. I could pretend it's not. I could pretend it's someone else and lose myself for a minute. Maybe then the pain would go away from losing Olivia.

Olivia.

What am I doing?

Just the thought of Olivia has me sobering. My eyes adjust and I see Addison more clearly now. Lifting her hand, I remove her from my crotch.

"There's no us anymore. You took care of that when you cheated on me."

"We were young. I was different."

"Addison," I warn as she moves to place her hand back on me. I grasp it in mine, halting her. "Don't do this. Don't do something you'll regret later. We have a good working relationship."

"We can have a better one." Her face is so close to mine her breath whispers against my cheek. "Can you imagine us together? We'd be unstoppable." And with that her lips find mine. Press against me.

Seeking entry.

CHAPTER THIRTY-FOUR

Olivia

Exposed: Move Over, Olivia Miller . . . Hello, Addison Price.

Word around town is our favorite CEO is out and about and he's not with his model girlfriend . . . or should we now say ex-girlfriend.

Sources close to Lancaster say he has officially reconciled with the heir to the Price Empire. It appears Spencer Lancaster has finally tossed the trash to the curb.

Fresh off the press, plus exclusive photos from their recent rendezvous.

We can't wait to report.

Through trembling limbs and salty tears, I examine the picture that has popped up on my iPhone. Like a glutton for punishment, weeks ago I had set it to notify me when a new post appeared. Now I wish I hadn't.

Denial would have been easier. But there is no denying this picture on my phone. He's back with her. We're done.

Sadness seeps into my veins as my chest tightens to the

point of pain. It feels like every last bit of air has been extracted from my lungs. Burning, ripping me apart. It soon morphs into something different. A disease, a venom, that spills into every molecule of my body, poisoning me. Strangling me. Making it hard to breathe.

I lost him.

She's beautiful. Perfect. Smart. Rich. A goddamn Mother Teresa. And what am I? I'm nothing. *A failure.* Not pretty enough. Not smart enough. Never enough.

I need something . . .

It hovers in me. Asking me to find peace, so I do. I'll search it out. I don't think as I leave my apartment. Not questioning what I'm doing. I just dial.

Me: Where are you?

I can still take it back. Turn around. But I don't want to. I need to escape and I know just where I can grab the solace I'm looking for.

It comes in the form of one word.

One text.

Sway.

By the time I arrive at Sway, the ache is too much to cope with. The need to escape creeps in my blood like a silent killer. Tormenting me. Beckoning me to find solace. I won't be able to escape it. It's unbearable. I'm being ripped in two with every breath I take. How could he do this to me?

How could I be this stupid? Think I'm enough for him. Think he'd want me. Anguish fills my veins. It's a black shadow. But I know this feeling . . .

It's hung over me before, and there is only one answer. I need to escape. I need to numb the voices. There is only one way to find peace . . .

Only one cure.

From across the room, I see my savior. Murph. When I approach him, his eyes are hollow, sunken in, and I know he has what I need. Déjà vu sweeps over me. It's so tragically beautiful being back here. I thought I had beaten it. Then I thought I could control it. But the need won out. The need to forgot. The need for the first rush to find me.

I lean into Murph. "Do you have any?" I whisper.

With one single nod, he pulls my hand. There is no pretense. He knows what I want, and he'll bring it to me. With quick steps, we walk into a private bathroom. When the door shuts behind us, he opens the vial. I can feel the nervous energy running rapidly within me. The weight of everything that has happened begins to crush me. How could I have been so stupid? How could I have thought I loved him? How could I have thought I had a chance at happiness? I've fought for so long to hold the hunger off. I have hated myself for being weak and succumbing, but why? It's so easy.

I lean forward over the plate he's laid the white powder on. It gleams at me with the brightness of the first snowfall on a bitterly cold day. Grabbing the bill from him, I lean down, close one nostril with my left hand and bring the bill to the opposite one. With a deep inhale, I feel my body kick back. My nose goes numb. My face goes numb. The familiar drip caresses my throat. Swiping my finger over the residue on the plate, I rub my fingers to collect it, then rub it over my gums.

In the mirror, I see my eyes are large and black and my mouth looks dry and cracked. It doesn't matter what I look like though. Nothing matters. This is easy. This is my calm. Everything will soon be okay.

I watch as he pulls out the plate and lays another line because it isn't enough. It's never enough until the voices go away. Until my insecurities are silenced.

I lean forward again. The fire and ice flow through my body. My heart beats warm blood through my veins. The cadence is drumming faster and faster as the high sets in. Then the beautiful numbness pounds through my brain. It enslaves me, controls every inch of me. But I need more. I can still feel the pain. The moment of relief is short-lived. I can feel it as it slithers away. As the image of Spencer and Addison skates through my mind.

I grab the vile from his hand and pour a heap directly on to my skin. I don't have the time to wait. I need it now. Only this will chase away the final remnants of my demons. The sounds in my brain are screaming at me that I have only been fooling myself. He was never mine. One more hit and it will be gone.

I feel the burn. I feel it as it seeps into every part of

my being. It morphs into rays of hope. I bask in the light. Anything seems possible. Murph pours another line. This is it. With this one, it will all be gone.

Inhale. The burn is stronger this time, causing sweat to break out across my brow. My vision becomes fuzzy. My heart smacks heavily against my chest. Pain grows. Pressure builds. My body begins to sway as the room spins on its axis. Then darkness takes over the light. Swirling blackness engulfs me. It brings the final oblivion. Stealing all that is left of me . . .

Consuming me entirely.

CHAPTER THIRTY-FIVE

Spencer

ALLOW IT.

I allow my lips to part, for her tongue to caress mine, for her hand to creep up my pants once again and stroke me through the fine material. I'm in too much shock to stop her, or maybe too drunk to know what I'm doing, but then finally the veil lifts and I push back.

"Addison, I'm with Olivia now."

"Not according to *Exposé*."

"You know better than to believe a tabloid." And then my own words come back to smack me in the gut. I know better than to read the papers. I should have listened to her. Given her a chance to explain. I owe her the benefit of the doubt.

"I need to go."

Addison moves to protest, but I glare at her and her mouth shuts, her eyes widening by the look I give her. Jumping up from the booth, I head out of the bar and straight for the elevator to take me down to the lobby. I try her phone, but the call won't connect. There's no service. Once in the lobby, I try again. This time it rings and rings. No answer.

Where is she?

I'm standing in the lobby pacing, contemplating my next move when Jack strides up to me, brows pinched, his jaw set. Something is wrong.

"What's going on?"

"A picture was leaked."

"What do you mean, leaked?"

"*Exposé* just posted a picture of you about fifteen minutes ago." He pulls out his phone and there I am from fifteen minutes earlier. Addison Price and me in a heated kiss.

Fuck.

"I need to find Olivia."

An hour has passed and there is no word from Olivia. I have called her phone half a dozen times and left three messages. I've just sent Jack to investigate when my phone rings. Olivia's name flashes across the screen.

"Olivia. I can explain."

"This isn't Olivia," a raspy male voice says through the phone. The muscles in my neck tighten at the sound of a man's voice using Olivia's phone.

"Who is this?" I grit out.

"It's Carson. I'm Lynn's boyfriend." Relief floods through me, but soon it devolves into pure panic.

"What the hell is going on?"

"Listen, man, I'm going to be straight with you. No one wants you here, but as a man who fucked up once and almost lost the girl I love, I'm risking a fight with Lynn to tell you. You need to get to the hospital. Olivia . . . well, I'm not sure how to say this—"

"Hospital? What the fuck are you talking about?"

"Shit, man. Olivia overdosed."

When the words hit my ears, I drop to the floor. I can feel the phone being lifted from my hands. Next thing I know I'm in my car and then Jack is ushering me into a hospital and I'm standing in front of her parents, her sisters.

"How is she?"

"Like you care?" her sister Bridget seethes at me. "Why are you even here? Shouldn't you be with your new girlfriend?"

"Bridget Miller." Her mother quiets her before placing her hands on her hips and turning to me.

"It was a misunderstanding. A terrible misunderstanding. Nothing happened. I love your daughter." And when the words slip out of my mouth I realize I do. I love Olivia Miller. Now I just need her to be okay, so I can tell her.

Olivia's mom lets out an audible sigh and then nods before gesturing to the vacant seat next to Carson. "You can sit if you want."

"Thank you. I'll just be right back." I need to get out of there for a minute. Before the walls close in around me. Before I lose my shit and start crying in front of these people.

When I'm finally alone, I bury my head in my hands and let it all loose. Every single emotion I've been holding on to. "Oh, God, please," I beg, looking up. "I'll do anything. I'll give up my entire fortune if you just keep Olivia safe." I hold on to those words and send them repeatedly to the man upstairs.

I only hope he doesn't turn his back on me.

CHAPTER THIRTY-SIX

Olivia

B*EEP*
Beep
Beep

The sound grates on my nerves. I flutter my lids to open my eyes, but trying causes more pain. My head is throbbing. I try to move my hand so I can rub my temples, but they don't move. Panic envelops me. Why can't I move? I concentrate on moving my fingers. I can't feel anything.

"Her eyes are squinting. She looks like she's in pain," a voice I recognize scolds someone else.

Who is that?

"I'll get the doctor," the stranger in the room offers.

"Please help her."

It's my mom. She's here. *Where is here?*

Those thoughts swirl in my head until I drift back into the black abyss. The next time I wake, I'm able to open my eyes. The blurry images in front of me slowly blink into existence. I'm in a room with white walls and machines everywhere.

A hospital.

I search the room for something recognizable, and that's when I see her curled in a ball in the corner on a chair. "Mom?" I manage to squeak. I press my hand to my mouth. My lips feel dry as if they are cracked and bleeding.

At the sound of my voice, she pops up. "Oh my God, Olivia. You're awake."

"Awake?"

"How do you feel? Are you okay?"

"Where am I?" I ask shakily.

"You're at University Medical Center. Y-You . . . You overdosed." Her voice breaks at the word overdosed. My mind scrambles to put the pieces together, to remember what happened. My muscles constrict when the memories flood back. The helplessness, the drugs, and then the calm.

"How long have I been here?" My voice cracks.

"You need something to drink. I'll see if I can get you some water."

I shake my head. "How long?"

"Twenty-four hours."

My vision blurs as tears threaten to spill. My chest constricts and I hate myself for being so weak. I hate myself for what I've become . . .

Again.

A few hours pass. Rain trickles down the windowpane. I can't help but stare, watching each drop of the murky water pour over the surface. Lost in my world, and in self-hatred.

A deep cough pulls my attention away, and my gaze sweeps to the door where the sound is coming from. Spencer stands there, his body stiff, unmoving. His chest is vibrating through deep breaths as he stares at me.

"Can I come in?" he finally asks, and my teeth gnaw at my lower lip as I think of something to say. I don't know where to start. I'm at a loss for words.

"I'm sorry. I'm so sorry." My words come out sheepish as tears prick the backs of my eyelids and then slowly trail down my cheeks. "You were right. I lied to you." My cold finger swipes across my face, wiping away the moisture that has collected. "I told you I stopped but it was a lie. I had, but then—"

Spencer takes a seat in the metal chair adjacent to my bed and places his hand on my arm.

"But then I started modeling. And then I saw the pictures. I couldn't handle it. I'm so sorry. I—"

"Olivia."

I shake my head and close my eyes tightly, not wanting to talk about it.

"Olivia. Open your eyes and look at me." His voice comes out more forceful than before. "I'm the one who's sorry. I turned my back on you. I should have let you explain, and then after all that—"

"Addison." I sniffle, closing my eyes and trying to stop the tears.

"It's not what you think."

I open my eyes wide. My heart pounds in my chest as I wait for an explanation. But as he takes a deep breath and exhales, I can't wait anymore. I need to know.

"Are you back together with her?" I hate how weak I sound. How unsure. How broken I am. A sickening feeling weaves its way inside me. I wouldn't be surprised if they were. They're perfect together.

"We are not—" he stops himself mid-sentence. "I shouldn't have let it go this far. I should have told you about our past and spoke to you about all the articles in *Exposé*. I should have reassured you. God, I'm not good at this."

"Good at what?"

"Relationships." My chin quivers but I don't speak. "I love you, Olivia. I love you so much it scares me."

My stomach drops as I let out a soft gasp. "You love me?" My voice is rough with emotion.

"Yeah." He nods while grabbing my hand and giving me a tight, sad smile. "I do."

My eyes close and after taking a deep breath, I reopen them and look into Spencer's eyes. His gaze is soft and full of emotion.

"I thought I lost you."

The pain in his gaze is evident. I feel my heart splinter into a million tiny pieces for everything I have done and for the pain I must have caused. The familiar itch spreads through my limbs.

"A part of me died when I heard you had overdosed. I can't live without you, Olivia. I need you to get better. I need you to be healthy. I think you should get help. Right now, you need to take care of yourself, heal. And when you're ready, I'll be there."

"You'd wait for me?" I whisper.

"I'd wait forever for you."

CHAPTER THIRTY-SEVEN

Olivia

A KNOCK AT THE DOOR HAS MY EYELIDS OPENING. My parents stand in the doorway looking like hell.

"Hi, Mom, Dad," I say weakly. "Hey guys," I whisper to my sisters.

My mother rushes to me, tears stream down her cheeks in black rivulets. "I-I was so scared. I just don't understand. Drugs? How did this happen? How did I not know?" I want to say it's because she's been busy with her own life, that and the fact that she doesn't read *Exposé*, but I don't.

I don't know what to say.

Seeing her cry breaks me. It feels like I'm being ripped in two. "I-I've been using on and off for a long time." My words cause her to sob even more.

"I-I don't understand," she stutters. "How could we not know? How could I not know? I'm your mother. Shouldn't I-I . . ." Her words get caught in her throat as she shakes uncontrollably.

"I got really good at hiding it," I mutter out. Swiping at her tears she lifts her head to meet my gaze. So I try to explain. "I was traveling for work. There's no way you could have known," I try to reassure her, but there is no calming her. Her daughter almost died. I almost died. "It started when I was still in college."

"When?"

"Junior year."

A gasp escapes Lynn's mouth. "It's my fault. That's when you found out about me. That's when you found out I was your sister."

"Lynn, it's not your fault." The words are hollow. It might not have been her fault, but I would be lying if I didn't believe that she was a catalyst. Tears start to pour down her face. Our father steps over to her and envelops Lynn in an embrace. I study his face. He looks older today. The lines that mar his face are evident and profound.

"I'm sorry," I whisper. "God, I'm so sorry."

His face softens and he takes my hand in his. "It's me who's sorry, Olivia. I failed you. And worse, I should've known what was going on. I failed you twice." A pent up sob releases through my mouth. "*Shh*," he coos, trying to calm me.

"What do I do now? I'm not sure how to do this? How to get better."

"We'll be here. We aren't leaving you. We'll help you find your strength and heal," he promises.

I might be broken and battered, but with my families help I know I can get through this.

I reach under my eyes and collect the gathering wetness with my fingertip. I focus my gaze on the ceiling, willing the tears to stop falling. I need to find the strength to be strong for them.

I need to find the strength to be strong for *me*.

Seventy-two hours later I'm released.

Spencer offers to drive me to the center, but instead, I tell him my parents will take me. I know they feel as if they're to blame for everything. It isn't their fault. Maybe the drama that came out was the catalyst, but in the end, I made my own choices.

The ride is uneventful. No one speaks. Dad's hand is holding Mom's, and with each strangled breath she takes, I can see his hand move, soothing her. It makes me feel awful, worse than I already feel for what I've put them through. If I had been stronger . . . better . . . enough.

I can't think like that. That's what got me into this. But it's innate. This feeling has been present in my life for so long, I don't know how to shut off the voices.

We arrive in Pennsylvania on Saturday morning. The early morning sun shining bright in the sky as we pull up. Thankfully, the rain has finally passed. "Wow," I mumble from the back of the car.

"It is beautiful," my mother agrees. "Hopefully, it helps you."

My eyes start to dampen. I shouldn't be thinking about how beautiful this place is. It shouldn't matter. The only thing that should matter is getting help.

We push open the door and soft music filters through the air. This place doesn't look like a rehab facility. All around me is peace and *tranquility*. It feels like I'm going on a relaxing vacation. Just like the name of the luxury rehab facility, Serenity. It is the perfect calming atmosphere to heal.

We walk farther into the lobby, and a man who looks to be my father's age strides over to us, followed by a younger woman who is closer to her mid-twenties. "Hello, you must be Olivia. I'm Dr. Andrews, and this is Charlotte. I'll be your psychiatrist for the duration of your stay here at Serenity, and Charlotte will be your program manager."

"Hi. These are my parents." I step back, allowing for introductions.

"It's a pleasure to meet all of you," Dr. Andrews says. "Follow me and we can briefly speak before Charlotte gives you the tour of the property." We follow Dr. Andrews into a reception area that looks like something out of a luxury resort. Two couches sit across from each other with a coffee table separating them.

"I'd like to explain a little about the facility. Here at Serenity, we treat both the physical and mental dependencies. If needed, we are capable of providing the *sufferer*," he smiles at me before he continues, "with a full detoxifi-cation program as well as all mental health aspects the suf-ferer will need to heal. While cocaine use usually doesn't lead to the same physical addictions as, say, other drugs, it can often lead to psychological withdrawal symptoms. Charlotte and I will work together to make sure that during your stay here we address and treat the underlying issues that led you down this path. How does that sound, Olivia?"

"Good." I nod. "It sounds good."

"Okay, great. I see here . . ." Dr. Andrews pauses as he looks down at the open file on his lap. "I see we have you signed up for a four-week commitment to address the addiction as well as any behavioral issues that might have contributed. At the end of the four-week time frame, you can always opt to stay longer. But if you choose to not continue after the thirty days, we will set you up in outpa-tient aftercare. This part is critical as recovery is a lifelong process."

We sit for a minute, my parents asking the necessary questions that I can't think to ask. I sign myself in, offi-cially registering for four weeks. Once all the paperwork is done, Dr. Andrews shakes my and my parents' hands before leaving us with Charlotte.

"How about that tour, and when we're done I'll show Olivia to her room?" Charlotte asks and we all nod as she leads us toward a set of double doors that must hold the treatment facilities.

"As Dr. Andrews previously said, here at Serenity we like to focus on what led to your addiction rather than solely the substance that brought you here to us. Our hope is to figure out where the addiction stemmed from and then reprogram the way you think, and heal you. Unlike other facilities, we offer mainly one-on-one therapy sessions. In these sessions, you'll work with Dr. Andrews to uncover the issues that led you to begin the use of cocaine. After we address the issue, we will help you to learn new coping mechanisms to deal with your stressors. When you leave the center, you will be equipped to handle them and will hopefully not have a relapse."

I nod. The rationale makes complete sense.

We continue to walk and Charlotte points to a room on the right as we continue our way down the hall. "These doors on your left, will bring you to our wonderful state-of-the-art spa. Also, in addition to the spa, we also have an array of specialized therapy programs you can take part in."

"Such as?" my dad asks.

"An example is art therapy. Participants who choose this can create a piece such as a drawing or sculpture. During the process, an art therapist will be present to guide you through the emotions, feelings and thoughts behind the work and how it relates to your life and your addiction. If art isn't for you, we also offer music therapy or nature hikes, as well as yoga and Reiki sessions." She pushes open a large glass door and we step inside. The room is vast and spacious. A group of women is doing yoga.

"This looks fantastic," my mom says. "How about phone privileges?" Apparently, my mom doesn't want to go a day without speaking to me.

"Great question. You will have limited access to your phone and Wi-Fi. Only for emergencies and if that happens, we like to be fully informed."

Am I really doing this?

Can I?

Yes. I can.

CHAPTER THIRTY-EIGHT

Spencer

With Olivia gone, and the Barcelona and now St. Barth's deals almost to completion, I have a lot of time on my hands to think.

Having watched the downward spiral Olivia went through shook me to my core. I need to do something about Pierce, and not just pay some money to make that shit go away. I need to decide what the hell is going on with him and get him help.

The strain with Grant doesn't help. My father is quiet about what went down that morning all those years ago, and Grant doesn't talk to any of us long enough to tell us, so it's time I get to the bottom of it.

I pick up the phone and I'm surprised when he answers since he's avoided my last dozen attempts. "We need to talk."

"I can't."

"Why did you do it? I thought we had a breakthrough." I sigh into the phone.

"Just because I told you about Dad, just because I was there at the hospital, doesn't mean anything has changed."

"But to fuck with my business? To fuck with the family business?"

"I don't want to talk about this. Go back to your perfect life with your perfect girlfriend and I'll get back to mine," he bites out.

"My perfect girlfriend. I just had to watch her struggle for her life, you asshole. Are you that spiteful?"

"I didn't know." His voice is low, remorseful.

"I know you didn't. She'll be okay, but having this happen made me realize a lot. I want my brother back. I didn't ask for this. I didn't ask for Dad to make me the CEO, nor did I tell him to disinherit you. You're hurting *me* by doing this. Your beef is with him, not me. I just want my brother back." I breathe. "Why won't you let me in? Tell me what happened?"

"I can't."

"Please." The phone goes silent for a minute and I wonder if he's hung up. "I don't want to lose you."

"I'll try."

And that answers my question. Maybe it won't be today when he opens up to me, maybe not tomorrow either, but this is a start and I'll take it.

———————◆———————

An hour later, I'm pulling up to the Lancaster compound

in Connecticut. The main house stands proud surrounded by rolling acres of green. Future plots of land for the Lancaster heirs.

I've never imagined building a house for myself there, but now I can envision it all in my head. A mixture of contemporary lines and elegant features; a marriage of designs. I can't wait to one day build it with Olivia by my side.

I shake my head. One day at a time. First she needs to get better. Then we can plan a future.

I drive down the long path to the main house and park my Aston Martin in the circular drive. When I reach the front door, I realize I didn't bring the spare key so I ring the bell and, surprisingly, my mother answers. Usually, a member of the staff does.

"Spencer," she says with a warm smile. The lines around her eyes grow deeper with worry. "What a nice surprise. We weren't expecting you."

"I need to speak to Dad."

"And you couldn't call first?"

"I couldn't run the risk of you or him putting me off."

"Oh." She doesn't say more, but I can tell she's concerned by the way she bites her lip. "This way. Your dad is resting in the library."

When I walk in, the air in my lungs leaves my body. My dad looks bad. Really bad. Old. Frail. "Hey, son." Even the sound of his voice is different from the man I grew up with. I don't know this man. "Everything okay?"

"Yeah, it's fine." I don't want to burden him anymore. But then I look more closely at him and realize that as with Olivia, or with her friend Lindsey, the future isn't clear. I'm lucky Olivia is still alive. That I have no regrets hanging over me. But can my dad say the same? Can Grant? If something were to happen to my dad or Grant, would the regrets of their pasts always haunt them? I decide then and there, no matter how frail he looks, we need to speak.

I take a seat and say what I came here to say. "Dad, you need to talk to Grant."

"And you need to mind your own business," he mumbles.

"No, I have stayed out of it long enough. I have let you tear this family apart, but not any longer. I love you, Dad, but this needs to end. I don't know what happened, and quite frankly, I don't care. It ends before we miss more of his life."

"I never told you not to have a relationship with your brother. That's on you."

"You're right, you didn't, but you sure as hell didn't help. Whatever happened left a toxic environment for everyone in the family, and eventually it eroded Grant's relationships with all of us. Fix it."

"I can't."

"You have to. Don't you want to meet your granddaughter?"

His face pales. "Of course I do."

"Then make it right."

"How?"

"That I can't tell you, but it's time you open your heart up. Be the bigger person and figure it out."

He doesn't speak for a minute then nods. He looks tired. Emotionally worn out from the exchange. After a minute I stand and take his hand. "I'm going to let you rest. Think about it." I lean down and kiss his forehead. "I love you, Dad."

I turn to walk away. "Spencer."

I look back at him.

"You make me real proud."

And for the first time in forever, I have hope for the Lancaster family.

CHAPTER THIRTY-NINE

Olivia

A WEEK HAS PASSED SINCE I ARRIVED HERE, AND today I find myself sitting across the room from Dr. Andrews.

"What made you decide to use cocaine?"

A part of me still doesn't want to answer. We've been tiptoeing around it, or at least I have, not wanting to admit my weakness, to confront it. Deep down I know this is necessary, though. I know saying the words will help me.

"I'm not skinny enough," I blurt out before I take a long, audible sigh. *That's not it*. Being skinny is not the reason I used coke, and if I was going to be healthy, I needed to be honest with him and with myself. Because this is about more than my weight. It's so much more than that.

"I'm not good enough. I've never been, and the drugs . . . They made it go away."

"Made what go away?"

"All of it."

"Olivia, I know this is a lot to talk about. It's okay if you aren't ready today. We don't have to figure everything out now. We can work up to it."

I think about it for a moment. If I were to say the words, I'd say . . .

I started the drugs at first to lose weight, but in truth, it was a way to escape how unhappy I was. It was a way to take control of my life when I felt as if it was flying out of control. I'd failed out of school. Family secrets had come out, and I didn't know how to cope. The modeling, the weight, the drugs were all things I could control. Or so I thought. But I'm not ready to face that yet, or at least not to find the words to tell him. So I nod and vow to try better tomorrow.

The next day comes, and I'm ready.

"How are you feeling today?"

"A little better."

"Are you ready to talk about why you started modeling?"

I am. "I was twenty-one, in my third year of school and I was failing, but I-I couldn't tell my parents. Instead, I told them I wanted to pursue this career choice."

"Why did you feel you couldn't tell them?"

"They were going through so much with Lynn. With discovering she was their daughter. I couldn't burden them. I wanted to excel at something. I'm not like the rest of my family, and I didn't know what else to do, but in the end, I failed at that, too. I failed at everything. I even failed at being a daughter."

"Did something happen to make you think that?"

"My father left. He left my mom, and he left me when I was a baby. Shouldn't he have stayed for me? Tried for me?"

"But he did."

"Yes, eventually. Or maybe he realized the grass is never greener. Maybe he didn't come back to be my father. Maybe he came back because he didn't want to be alone."

"Have you ever discussed what happened with your dad?"

"Why would I? It doesn't change anything."

"But it does, Olivia. Don't you see? When did the drugs start?"

"When I started modeling."

"And when was that?"

"When I found out. What are you saying? Are you saying this all stems from my parents?"

"You just told me you weren't enough, right? That you used drugs because you felt inadequate."

"And you're saying this started when I found out the truth."

"Your first thought, the first thing you said was that you weren't enough to make your father stay. I think it would be good for your healing if we had your father join us. Would you be okay with that?"

I nod, still trying to wrap my head around the idea that something so small could be so influential in my life.

"Olivia, I'd like you to work on a few things today

before we meet again tomorrow."

"Okay."

"First, I'd like to see when your dad is available to come, to join us for one of your therapy sessions. But before that, I'd like you to write down your triggers. Words, feeling, and thoughts, so we can discuss them."

My scheduled appointment isn't for fifteen minutes, but I need the minute to calm my nerves. The idea of finally asking my father all the unanswered questions hangs on me. I've never confronted the issue. I simply buried my head in the sand, pretending his previous actions didn't haunt me.

Until now.

Now, there's no more hiding. Dr. Anderson is right. If I don't confront this demon, I'll never actually be cured. It's time to heal.

When I step inside the room, the air in my lungs leaves my body in shock. Dad's already here. He's sitting down, his head in his hands, but when he hears the door hit the wall, his head pops up. He looks tired as if the weight of the world rests on his shoulders.

I did this to him.

This pain he harbors is *my* fault.

I don't even make it a step within the room before I'm pulled into his arms. His embrace wraps around me, comforting me.

"Daddy . . ."

"Sweetie." He hugs me tighter, and I start to shake in his grasp. Every pent up emotion is bubbling to the surface until the dam finally breaks and tears spring from my eyes.

"Why?" I ask between croaked sobs escaping my throat. I pull back, looking into my father's eyes. His broken eyes. "Why did you leave me? Why wasn't I enough for you to stay?"

"It wasn't your fault, Olivia. It was never your fault. It had nothing to do with my love for you." A tear runs down my father's face. "I was a different man then. I was selfish, but it never meant I didn't love you. When I thought I was losing you and your mom, I came back. I begged and pleaded to come back, because leaving you was the biggest mistake of my life. I have always loved you, Olivia. You will always be my little girl. Never doubt that. Ever."

I'm not sure how long we stand there in each other's arms before Dr. Anderson walks in, but when I pull away, it feels as if a burden has been lifted off me. I had never realized how much I needed to hear him tell me it wasn't my fault, but now that he has, peace falls over me.

I'm lighter.

Content.

Free.

—————————•◦•——————————

As the weeks pass and the sessions continue, I start to

realize so much about my family and myself. Being able to talk to my dad and finally hear what happened was healing and helped me move forward.

Sometimes everything needs to fall apart before you can rebuild and construct a stronger foundation.

I learned that the hardest and also the most important thing is learning to love myself.

I'm still working on that. Day by day, I love myself more and more. It's been a long time since I believed I deserved love. For years I clung to this, too scared that I wasn't enough, too afraid to fail. But I'm not scared anymore.

I'm ready to move on.

———————

The week I'm scheduled to leave, Dr. Andrews is sitting across from me, notebook in hand. He places it down on the coffee table and leans forward. "So what do you want to do now? You stated last session you no longer want to model. That it's a stressor for you. So now that modeling is out of the question do you have any ideas what you want to do?"

"I'm not sure what my options are?"

"Well, tell me something you feel passionate about?"

"That no one goes through what I went through."

"What do you mean?"

"The drugs, self-doubt. The dieting. I realize now just how toxic being a model was for me."

"What would you do if you could go back and talk to your former self?"

"I would tell her she was beautiful on the inside and out. I'd like to go up to the model who gave me that bump so many weeks ago and say why? And I'd like to tell the photographer I don't need to be sick to be beautiful. I already am."

"So why don't you?"

"What do you mean?"

"There has to be an advocacy group for them. You can look into finding a job there."

"No. I could never."

"Why not?"

"I . . ." I stare at him for a minute trying to put into words my insecurities. My doubts. "I don't think I'm strong enough to work in the industry. I need to do something simple."

"Like what, Olivia?" He inclines his head as he waits for me to answer.

"I could go back to school and become a . . ." My words travel off as I try to think of a career. But nothing of interest comes to mind. "I could open a boutique. I like clothes."

"Would that make you happy?"

"I don't think so," I admit on a sigh.

"Then I don't think you should do it. I don't think you should do anything you aren't passionate about."

"I just don't think I'm—"

"You are strong enough. You conquered your addiction not only physically but also mentally. You've come so far. You've grown so much. If any one can do this, it's you. Believe in yourself, Olivia."

And in that moment . . .

In my weakness, I find my strength.

CHAPTER FORTY

Olivia

THIRTY DAYS . . .

Thirty long, *hard* days.

Thirty day of learning who I am, and healing parts of myself that I didn't even know were broken.

In my short time at Serenity Dr. Anderson helped me rebuild my foundation. Because if the foundation is strong everything else can be fixed.

That's what I did, and now, whatever the future will bring, I know I'll be just fine. I finally learned to love myself, scars and all. I'll never be that perfect person. I'll always be a little bit flawed, and that's okay. Those flaws make me who I am. They aren't marring my skin. Instead they are making me . . . me.

I'm back in the city. It's a day earlier than expected, but I was in such a rush to get home it didn't even dawn on me to call first. I'll just have my parents drop me at The Lancaster.

When I walk in the front door, the concierge greets me.

"Is Mr. Lancaster home?" I really should have called first to check, but I was too frazzled.

"No, but when he was walking out, he said he'd be back in five minutes. I'll have George show you to the suite."

Once inside, I nervously pace. I pick up my cell to dial him, the anticipation of surprising him growing too strong. I need to tell him I'm here. I need to see him.

As I'm about to dial the door opens, but I hear two voices and one is a girl. They grow louder as they turn the corner and enter the room. That's when I see it's Spencer. And he's with Addison.

His mouth drops. Caught like a deer in headlights. "Olivia?"

I feel sick.

"I guess forever came too soon," I say under my breath. I pick up my bag to go.

"What do you mean?"

"You said you'd wait."

"I did. I am!"

"Sure looks that way," I hiss, but then I realize I'm doing just what he did—not giving him the benefit of the doubt. It's easy to fall back on old habits. I take a breath, but as I'm about to say his name, he grabs my face.

"Will you shut up already," he growls. And then he's kissing me.

"I-I should be going," I hear from behind me, but neither of us breaks away to answer her.

In the background, the door opens and shuts.

"I love you," he says against my lips.

"I love you too."

"I can't wait another minute," he growls through kisses.

Hand and hand we walk into the bedroom until I'm standing at the foot of the bed and Spencer appraises me. He drops to his knees and pushes my panties down my thighs, and I push forward toward his hand. The rough pads of his fingers tease my sensitive skin.

Desperate for his touch, my hips tilt to meet the warmth of his caress.

To increase the pressure.

To beg him to touch me, to fill me.

My body starts to quiver as I wait, and then when the need is all encompassing, he pushes inside and then up-ward with his fingers, finding the sensitive spot buried deep within.

Spencer brings me so close, but when I'm teetering on the brink, he pulls back, strips off his clothes and begins to stroke himself.

I lay back, positioning my legs farther apart to allow him to cradle between them.

My chest heaves in as I wait. Then slowly Spencer pushes inside me, and our bodies come together.

He thrusts in and out, each move stronger than the last.

We move together as if we are one being. Spencer's breath caressing my lips as he makes me his over and over again.

The next morning we're lying in bed and I realize we have so much to say to each other. There's so much he's never told me, and if we want to move forward, it's time he lets me in. I know we need to talk, but we won't be able to do it here. Getting up from the bed, I walk to the bathroom and start to brush my teeth and freshen up. Once done, I pop my head through the door.

"Want to go for a walk?"

"Now?"

"Yeah." He doesn't ask why, but I imagine he knows we have a lot to talk about. So without another word, he starts to dress as well.

An hour later, we're in Central Park. It's eerily quiet for this time of day. As if we are the only people in the park, the only people in the city. We're in our own snow globe and I hope this conversation won't rattle our peaceful world.

"So, tell me what happened?" I ask, turning my head to look at him from where we're perched on a small bench.

His brow furrows. "What happened? What do you mean?"

"I know you were having issues with work but we never talked. You never told me what really happened. You kept me at a distance, never letting me in. Why you were so cold and distant sometimes?"

"I was never cold and distant with you." He pauses and looks me in the eyes. His normally vibrant green eyes look dull and tired. "Was I?" His jaw tightens as realization hits him.

"Only a few times, but although you might not have snapped often, I could still sense it. When you would walk into a room. When you got off the phone. I could feel the chill. Every time."

"I'm sorry. I didn't know." He runs his hands through his unruly hair.

"So tell me what happened?"

"My brother Grant happened." He frowns.

"I don't understand?"

Spencer looks up to the early morning sky, takes a deep breath and then meets my stare. "Then I guess I should start from about five years ago. Well, as you know my father wanted to retire.

"It was always assumed that Grant would take over. I didn't initially want to go into the business in this manner. I had other dreams." His eyes look lost. Like he's remembering the life he had before The Lancaster.

"Architecture."

He nods.

"Grant loved the business. He was ruthless like Dad, and loyal, but also stubborn like Dad."

"Sounds a little like another brother I know." I smile.

"I'm not sure the exact details because Dad doesn't want to talk about Grant, and Grant . . . well, Grant cut us off. There was a major falling out so big that Dad not only stripped him of his chance at running The Lancaster, but also changed his will."

I gasp at this information. "Oh my God. What did he do?"

"Well, Grant's trust had already kicked, so he has plenty of money, but all he wanted was The Lancaster when Dad retired shortly after the fight and named me the CEO that was the end. Until that point, Grant and I still spoke, but after I was appointed it was like he was dead. He dropped completely out of the public realm for many years, but about a year ago he resurfaced. He had purchased property and announced he was opening the L. The L is in complete competition with our brand. Basically, it's a big giant fuck you to me and my family."

"But I don't understand why is this affecting you now? Hasn't this been going on for years?"

"Remember when we met?"

"Obviously."

"I wasn't supposed to be in London. I had flown into Manchester to do a deal. The deal fell through. Someone outbid me, so I changed plans and went to London, and from there you know what happened. But then, when I returned to the States, I put in some interest in a property in the Caribbean and I was outbid again. I had Jack look into it, and I bet you can't guess who was behind it."

My mouth falls open. "Oh my God. Was it Grant?"

"Yeah, what Jack found out was that Grant was bidding on every property I wanted."

"That's horrible."

"The worst part is I thought we were making progress, but who the fuck knows with Grant."

"So what happened? You obviously got the properties."

"No, that's where Addison stepped in. She sold me the property in Barcelona and the property in St. Bart's."

The sound of her name makes me shake, and Spencer pulls me into his lap and kisses my forehead. "It's only been you, Olivia. Only you."

"I know nothing happened. It just makes me remember what I did." I try to move away from him.

"Don't distance yourself from me. That's why this all happened, I didn't tell you the issues I was having with Grant and you didn't tell me about the pressure you were under. I'm not sure why we both didn't have the strength to fully open up to one another, but we can't go back there. We need to be honest with each other in order for this to work."

"Okay."

"Promise me."

"I promise."

He kisses my lips.

"Good girl."

"I can show you just how good I can be," I purr.

"I'll take you up on that." And with that, all words are stopped, and his mouth descends again.

———————•◦•———————

A few weeks have passed and we have settled into a comfortable relationship. I still have an apartment, but I'm pretty much living with Spencer at The Lancaster these days.

"Goddamn it," I mumble to myself.

"What?"

"I can't find shit," I say, closing my computer and finishing my Google search.

"Nothing? Really?"

"Nothing. Fuck. Now what am I going to do?"

"Start your own."

"I can't start my own." He raises an eyebrow. "Wait, you're serious aren't you?"

"Olivia, if this is what you want, then do it. Start your own modeling agency. One that has the models interest at heart, not money. Be an advocate for these girls. Show them, teach them."

"I don't know a thing about—"

"You know a lot more than you think. You were in the business for how many years?"

"Over two."

"You know models, photographers, you have contacts at brands and magazines and the ones you don't have, I do."

"How would I even start? I'd have to take out a loan," I mutter to myself, trying to think of a way to do this. It actually would be a dream come true.

"I would finance you."

"I could never let—"

"Stop right there. There's nothing to let. I love you. I believe in you. I want to invest in you."

"I could never take money from you." We sit there at an impasse, but he knows I won't budge.

"Would you take a zero interest loan?" *Would I? Can I do that?*

If it's not a handout . . .

If I pay him back?

"I could ask my parents. They have the money."

"Olivia, you're being ridiculous. Why bother them? They still have graduate school for Bridget, and possibly medical school for Lynn. Let me help you."

"I'd have to pay you back."

"Of course."

"What if I fail?"

"You won't," he says forcefully, full of conviction.

"But what if I do? None of them, not Lucinda, Helen, or Giorgio or Bennett, thought I'd make anything of my life."

"Prove them wrong."

He's right, and I will do just that. I will prove them wrong. I will prove all of them wrong.

———————•◦•———————

I stretch my arms above my head and let out an audible yawn. Spencer and I have been sitting on his couch for the last few hours with my legs draped over his as he speaks on the phone. *Working*. I, however, am reading a book on my Kindle. It's Sunday, and unlike Spencer, I don't work on Sundays. I guess once the agency is officially opened, I might be singing a different tune, but until then, I'll snuggle up against him and enjoy his company.

From the corner of my eye, I see him put his phone down and turn to look at me. "Come on," he says as he lifts my legs off his and moves to stand.

"Where?"

His lips tip up in a smirk. "I have a surprise for you."

"Do you?" I toy with a lock of my hair to appear flirtatious, and he laughs.

"I do. But not that kind of surprise." He gently encases my hand in his and pulls me up.

"Should I change?" When I look down at what I'm wearing, I'm horrified. Beat up black leggings that are so faded they appear gray and an oversized thermal.

"Not at all. You're perfect." Even in my current state of clothing disarray, when he says it, I believe it. I *feel* it. I feel like I've walked the gates of hell and made it out to the other side. Who cares what I'm wearing, as long as I'm happy. And these days, I am.

"Do I get a hint?"

"I hope you're hungry."

With that, my stomach decides to growl as if on cue. "That's the only hint I get?"

"Yep."

"Can't wait," I deadpan, but Spencer knows I'm excited. These last few months he's learned everything about me. From every insecurity to all aspects of my sense of humor.

Hand and hand, we make our way out of the suite, which has officially become his private residence. He redecorated it to live there full-time so we could spend more time together. It's warm and cozy now. Each piece of furniture picked for our comfort rather than luxury. He even asked my opinions, wanting to make sure I always felt at home here and I do.

When we make it down the elevator and out of the building, we're greeted by George the doorman.

"Would you like me to have your driver come—"

"That won't be necessary. It's a beautiful night."

And it is. Summer has turned to fall, and fall is my favorite time in the city. The air is crisp and smells of cinnamon spice and toasted nuts.

"It's only a few blocks," Spencer informs me.

Together we walk in perfect pace with one another. Comfortable. Like we've done this a million times, and in truth we have. Since I've been back from rehab, Spencer and I are rarely apart. Sure, I'm busy getting my agency set up, and he's busy expanding, but when we're not working, we are always together.

After about a ten-minute walk, we cross over Third Avenue, and Spencer stops in front of a small awning. He swings the door open, and there is a set of weathered stairs leading to a small intimate restaurant. There are no frills about the space, and the restaurant appears stuck in a time warp from the seventies. The furniture is old and dated, and soft music plays throughout the interior. The restaurant is not what I expect from Spencer Lancaster, but this man constantly surprises me.

Spencer leads us to a table in the corner and then lifts his arms to wave at a man coming out of the kitchen. We sit in comfortable silence as we wait for the waiter to approach the table. Spencer takes my hand in his, his fingers tracing circles on my own as he stares into my eyes lovingly, a gesture that makes me warm and fuzzy inside. He's openly tender, never letting me doubt how he feels about me.

"Olivia, this is Nino," Spencer introduces me once the waiter approaches our table. "He's the owner and genius who will be preparing our food."

"Such a pleasure to meet you," I say extending my free hand to shake his.

"The pleasure is mine, *bellissima*."

"Knock it off, old man," Spencer chides, and Nino's aged face cracks into a flirtatious smile as he winks at me. It's obvious Spencer has known Nino awhile. "No menus tonight, Nino. Whatever you want to make, we'll eat."

As Nino walks away, Spencer turns to face me again. "This is my favorite Italian restaurant in the city. I've been coming here since I was a kid. As far back as I can remember, we used to do Friday night dinner here."

"So how come I'm only now finding out about it?"

"I don't know . . ." Small lines appear on Spencer's forehead. He looks around. His gaze is distant, lost in a memory. "This place reminds me so much of a different time, but I like having you here."

"Well, I like being here with you."

"I'd like to make it a tradition. That's what it was to me, but I want to change it to us. To you and me."

"You mean that?"

"This is what I want my future to look like—you and me starting new traditions *together*. I want to do it all with you. When you're strong, when you're weak, I want to be with you. I can't promise to not be an asshole, but I don't want us to miss any experiences."

"I feel as if I'm living in a fairy tale," I whisper.

"No fairy tale. This is all real, Olivia. You deserve this and so much more."

EPILOGUE

Olivia

'M STANDING ON THE PIECE OF PROPERTY THAT SPENCER purchased in Antibes. A year has passed, but it's still as beautiful as the day he first brought me here. The water is crystal blue and the skies are even more brilliant in color.

This past year I went to hell and back, but I've gained back my strength. I've spent my days launching my agency, my nights with Spencer, and any extra free time helping Lindsey.

Lindsey is still in recovery. She can walk now but requires the use of a cane. Thankfully, she lives close to me and I see her on a daily basis. Most days I accompany her to physical therapy.

She's here with the rest of our friends and family. We're all at the property, waiting for the ribbon cutting that will officially begin the groundbreaking for the newest Lancaster Hotel chain, Lancaster International. I'm so proud of Spencer. He's made his dream a reality and has taken Lancaster Hotels into the next generation. He stands in front of us all, proud and visibly excited. He's ready to give his speech. A hush falls over the crowd as he raises his hand to quiet everyone. He takes in a deep breath, and the first signs of nerves cross over his face.

Strange. Spencer is never nervous.

"Thank you all for coming," he begins with a commanding tone, able to hush the last of those talking. "I'm so proud to be standing here today, ready to embark on the next chapter in my life." He looks at me and gives me a breathtaking smile. "I wish I could take credit for this purchase, but in all honesty, it was a very special woman who showed me just how valuable this piece of property was. Olivia, would you come up here, please?"

I look around questioningly. *Is he serious?*

Everyone around me nods his or her head, so I stand and walk up to him. He grabs my hand in his and pulls me into his side.

"A year ago I stood on this very piece of land with Olivia by my side, and at that time I was still contemplating whether I should purchase it for the next brand of luxury hotels. It was Olivia who told me she'd never build a hotel on this land." He chuckles, shaking his head.

"At that time I thought she was crazy. All I could see were dollar signs. Potentially, billions would be lost by not jumping on that purchase. If I didn't snatch it up, someone would. I asked her what she'd do if she owned it, and she told me she'd make it a private residence." He looks at me and smiles. "She said she'd build her home here so she could wake up every day to this view. At that time, I thought it was nonsense. Why waste such a valuable piece of property just to build a house on it? The past year I've spent with her made me understand what she was saying. The quiet solitude and the remarkable beauty that is this land shouldn't be tainted by industry of any sort."

I scrunch my nose in confusion at his words.

"Today we're not here to celebrate the next generation of Lancaster Hotels, but the next generation of Lancasters."

My head jerks to him and he smirks. "Well . . . hopefully." He pulls a small snow globe from his pocket. It doesn't look like any snow globe I've ever seen. It's completely custom, and the words etched on the side say *home*. Inside is a beautiful house sitting on a mountain with the ocean as the backdrop.

What the heck is going on?

When I turn back to Spencer, he's down on one knee. It takes me a second, but I finally know what's going on. I gasp in shock.

"Olivia Miller, I've loved you since the day I saw you. I might not have known it then, but I absolutely know it now. The best decision I've ever made was asking you to escort me to Vence. That day changed my life."

I begin to cry. His words are so beautiful and I see the sincerity in his eyes. He loves me as much as I love him.

"I've brought our friends and family here today to ask you to be my wife. Build a home right here, somewhere we can wake up every morning together and see exactly what you envisioned. Will you marry me and help make this our home?"

I fall to my knees in the sand, unable to catch my breath. Everything I've ever wanted in life is being thrown at my feet and the emotions are overwhelming. This man has been my rock the past year. We may have had some miscommunication issues, and we may have a long road ahead of us, but ultimately he's what I want forever and he's giving it to me. There's only one thing I can possibly say in this moment.

"Yes."

He envelops me in his arms and we fall to the sand as everyone around us cheers happily.

"I love you, Olivia. More than life itself."

"I love you, Spencer. Always."

Our life is chaos, constantly being hounded by the press, but in the end, nothing they say can rock us. We've built something strong and solid.

A foundation for the future.

ACKNOWLEDGMENTS

I want to thank my entire family. I love you all.

Thank you to my husband and my kids for always loving me, I love you so much!

Thank you to my Mom, Dad, Liz and Ralph for always believing in me, encouraging me and loving me!

Thank you to my in-laws for being so cool about me writing books and encouraging it!

Thank you to all of my brothers and sisters!

Thank you to everyone that helped with Clandestine.

Write Girl Editing Services

Indie After Hours

Lawrence Editing

Becca Mysoor

Love N. Books

Marla Esposito

Champagne Book Design

Hang Le

Lori Jackson

Mila Grayson

Becca Zsurkán

Thank you Give Me Books.

Thank you Rafa Catala and Fabian Castro

Thank you to my beta team! Leigh, Mia, Willow, Melissa, Christine. Thank you for your wonderful and extremely helpful feedback.

Thank you to my agent Emily Sylvan Kim and everyone

at Prospect for believing in me!

Thank you to my translators ;-) Sophie Broughton, Maïwenn blogs, Mom.

I want to thank ALL my friends for putting up with me while I wrote this book. I know it's no easy task! Trish, Lisa, Paige, Serena . . . Thank you!

Thank you to my smut moms!

Thank you to my Phi Girls for always being there!

Thank you to Melissa Saneholtz. You are my sanity! There aren't enough ways for me to say THANK YOU!

Mia you are my plotting goddess, I love how your brain works. I couldn't have gotten through this book without your help!

Leigh . . .I could never have written Spencer without you or this book! Thank you for your endless cheerleading and support.

Livia . . . Dude, I don't know why you answer my calls when you know I'm writing but thank you!

To all of my author friends who listen to me bitch and let me ask for advice, thank you!

Melody, Corinne, Celia, AL, Lauren

To my *Exposé* sisters, I loved getting to be part of this amazing project with you.

Willow, Adrianna, Mandi, Frankie, Mia

Thank you to all the ladies I sprint with! I would never have finished this book without you pushing me.

To the ladies in the Ava Harrison Support Group, I couldn't have done this without your support!

Please consider joining my reader group if you haven't: http://bit.ly/2e67NYi

Thanks to all the bloggers! Thanks for your excitement and love of books!

Last but certainly not least . . .

Thank you to the readers!

Thank you so much for taking this journey with me.

For future release information please sign up here to be alerted: http://bit.ly/2fnQQ1n

BY AVA HARRISON

Imperfect Truth

Through Her Eyes

trans-fer-ence

Illicit

ABOUT THE AUTHOR

Ava Harrison is a New Yorker, born and bred. When she's not journaling her life, you can find her window shopping, cooking dinner for her family, or curled up on her couch reading a book.

Connect with Ava

Newsletter Sign Up: http://bit.ly/2fnQQ1n

Facebook Author Page: http://bit.ly/2eshd1h

Facebook Reader Group: http://bit.ly/2e67NYi

Goodreads Author Page: http://bit.ly/2eNjYwX

Instagram: http://bit.ly/2f5H5RT

BookBub: https://www.bookbub.com/authors/ava-harrison

Amazon Author Page: http://amzn.to/2fnVJHF